Praise for

Christmas at the Palace

'Huge **fun** with a slightly different slant.
Thoroughly enjoyable'
KATIE FFORDE

'Written with a sure touch, and Jeevani's characters leap
from the page. I **love** Jeevani Charika's writing!'
SUE MOORCROFT

'What a **fantastic** and **fascinating** read. A **refreshingly
different** and thought-provoking romance'
PHILLIPA ASHLEY

Jeevani Charika is British–Sri Lankan. She started off in the south of England, then spent her childhood living in places as diverse at Sri Lanka, Nigeria and Micronesia before settling down in Yorkshire, where she now lives with her husband and two daughters.

Jeevani also writes romantic comedies and women's fiction under the name Rhoda Baxter. Her books have been shortlisted for the RoNA awards, the Love Stories awards and the Joan Hessayon award. She is a member of the UK Romantic Novelists' Association and the Society of Authors.

A microbiologist by training, she loves all things science geek. She also loves cake, crochet and playing with Lego. You can find out more about her (and get a free book) by signing up to her newsletter on her website: http://jeevanicharika.com/

Christmas at the Palace

Jeevani Charika

ZAFFRE

First published in Great Britain in 2018 by
ZAFFRE PUBLISHING
80–81 Wimpole St, London W1G 9RE
www.zaffrebooks.co.uk

A CIP catalogue record for this book is
available from the British Library.

ISBN: 978-1-78576-818-7

Also available as an ebook

1 3 5 7 9 10 8 6 4 2

Typeset by IDSUK (Data Connection) Ltd
Printed and bound in Great Britain by Clays Ltd, Elcograf S.p.A.

Zaffre Publishing is an imprint of Bonnier Zaffre,
part of Bonnier Books UK
www.bonnierzaffre.co.uk
www.bonnierbooks.co.uk

while the boy took cover by her wall of newspaper clippings.

'What are all these for?'

'I'm a reporter.'

He looked at her doubtfully. 'Really? You're pretty young.'

Lil tucked her hair behind her ears and then untucked it again. 'I'm older than you.'

'Are any of these by you?'

Lil tried avoiding the question with another snort that she hoped would sound like 'what do you think?' But the boy just looked at her blankly so she straightened up and said, 'Not yet . . . but one day you'll see my name in print.'

'Oh,' he said.

'I'm waiting for a big story.' Lil felt as though things had got switched around somehow. It was time to turn the tables. She was sucking in a big mouthful of air to do just that when he spoke again.

'I have a story for you. It's a Missing Persons case.'

Lil let the breath escape. 'Really? All right, I'll bite. Who's missing?'

The boy turned to face her, his gaunt face shaded with grey. 'I am.'

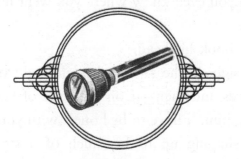

Chapter 3

Nedly

Lil nodded to the red plastic swivel chair by her desk and the boy sat gingerly on the edge of it.

'OK, pal, spill the beans.' She turned her Anglepoise lamp on him and stood behind it, a silhouette behind the shade. 'Who is missing you?'

He blinked at her. 'I – I don't know.'

Lil noticed that under the strong light the boy's skin was so pale it was almost translucent. 'You don't remember?'

He shrugged.

'Do you even know where you went missing from?'

He shook his head.

Lil sighed. She swung the lamplight out of his eyes and then sat on the edge of her bed facing him. 'I have to be honest with you; this isn't shaping up to be much of a story. It sounds to me like a bad case of amnesia. Maybe you should just hand yourself in at a police station or a hospital, see if anyone is looking for you?'

The boy looked down. 'I tried that. No one took any notice.' The shadows in the room lengthened around him. 'I just need someone to help me find out what happened. I thought you seemed like the sort of person to help someone, if they could.' He turned his bush-baby eyes on her, full beam, and then dropped his gaze to the floor. 'Maybe I was wrong.'

He wasn't wrong: Lil was that person, but an amnesia case wasn't going to get her onto the pages of the *Klaxon*. That didn't mean she felt good about it. She tried out a little white lie. 'I have a lot on my plate at the moment; there's this big case I'm working on –'

The boy interrupted, beaming, 'Is it to do with that lost toy?'

'Ha!' Lil tried to humph it off. 'What makes you think I've got time to go looking for toys?'

'I saw you take the flyer.'

'Well . . . Yeah,' she admitted. 'That is one of the cases I'm working on at the moment. But obviously it's not the main one.'

'Of course,' he continued respectfully. 'But, anyway, I was thinking, maybe I could help – with your case – in return for your help. Sort of like a payment.'

'You want to be my sidekick?'

'No,' he said, faintly discouraged. 'I was thinking more like a partner . . .'

Lil ignored him. She rubbed the sleep out of one eye thoughtfully. 'I hadn't thought about taking on a sidekick before, but maybe I could use one. Can you take photographs?'

'Not really. I mean, no.'

'Oh.' Lil was disappointed. 'So what can you do?'

He shrugged.

'Are you any good at sneaking around?'

His face brightened. 'I would say I'm pretty good actually. I got in here without anyone seeing me, didn't I?'

'OK,' said Lil, her mind humming with the possibilities. 'You might come in handy. Missing Peoples is not really my line of work but I'll take your case and in return you can help me with mine. Deal?' She spat on her hand and held it out to him. He didn't take it. 'It's only a bit of spit.' Lil rolled her eyes and wiped her hand on her dressing gown. 'OK, I'll just have to take your word for it. Deal?'

'Deal,' the boy said, and for the first time since they met Lil saw the flicker of a smile cross his face.

'So, have you got a name, at least?

His gaze dropped to the floor. 'I don't remember that either.'

'You're a tough nut to crack but if you're

going to be my sidekick I'm going to have to call you something.'

He frowned, letting his eyes wander around the room as though he was trying to find his name hidden there amongst Lil's things.

'I thought maybe I might be called . . . something like . . .' He lowered his voice. 'I think I might be . . . Ned.' His face drained of what little colour it had. 'But that can't be right, it sounds so . . .'

'You think you're Ned?'

His eyes grew wide, the pupils blooming into fathomless tunnels. Lil had to tear her gaze away from them, suddenly afraid of what she might see there. The boy shuddered and the bulb in the Anglepoise blew, leaving them in semi-darkness. Lil watched a thin curl of metallic smoke trickle out of the lamp and into the path of the moonlight. She shivered and then swallowed back the creeps.

When the boy finally spoke his voice was barely a whisper. 'I don't like the sound of that at all.'

'Maybe that's not your name then?'

'I can't remember. I thought it was Ned, but maybe it's just something like that.'

'Ted? Ed?'

He looked at her searchingly. 'I don't like the sound of any of those.' He went paler still. 'No, I don't like the sound of them at all. It's like N-Ned, but not as final.'

'Nedward? Neddo? Nedly?'

'Nedly,' he said quickly. 'That's my name.'

Lil folded her arms. 'I made that name up.'

'Well, until I remember my real name I'll stick with that one.'

Lil puckered her brow and tried to stop a yawn escaping. 'Well, Nedly, someone must be missing you.'

'I hope so,' he said, unconvinced.

'Don't worry, we'll find them. Tomorrow.' This time she let the yawn out full force with an accompanying groan. Nedly didn't seem to get the hint. He just sat there at Lil's desk, his skin palest blue in the moonlight. 'So . . . tomorrow then? Which means you should go now and come back *tomorrow*. We'll start work on your case then.'

'Oh, OK.' Nedly said, but he still didn't go anywhere.

'Nedly, you can't sleep here.' He looked down. Lil sighed. 'I suppose I could wake Mum up and ask her if you can kip on the settee.'

'No,' said Nedly. 'Don't wake anyone. I'll go.' He walked over to the door. 'Can you see me out?'

Lil opened the door for him; as he passed her she shivered. 'Did you leave a window open somewhere?' He didn't answer. She followed him down the stairs; Lil knew how to dodge the steps that creaked, but Nedly just seemed to avoid them. At the front door he waited again for her to open it. 'You know, next time,' she told him, 'you should just knock like everyone else.'

Chapter 4

Satsumas Don't Lie

The next morning Lil woke late.

'Lil!' Her mum shouted her name up the stairs. 'LIL!'

'Coming!' Lil yelled back. Stopping at the airing cupboard to get some fresh clothes, she opened the door. Her jeans were in a pile on the floor.

She frowned. No, not her jeans: these had scuffed old trainers at the end of them. These jeans had legs inside them. Black eyes stared up at her out of a ghostly white face. She screamed. Crouching beneath the bottom shelf and the hot water tank was Nedly.

Panic darted across Nedly's face. 'Sorry, I –' His voice was drowned out by the sound of footsteps pounding the stairs as Lil's mum hurtled onto the landing.

Lil turned to face her, slamming the door in Nedly's face.

Lil's mum, Naomi, was slight and bespectacled with the same large cup-handle ears as Lil. She gave Lil an exasperated look. 'I've been calling you for ages! Are you OK?' Lil nodded dumbly. 'Good. Breakfast is nearly ready – scrambled eggs on toast! Come on.'

As soon as the coast was clear Lil reopened the door. The airing cupboard looked empty. Cautiously prising apart towels and bundles of clothes she peered round the back of the hot-water tank. 'Nedly?' she whispered. 'Are you there?' Wooden planks lined the back wall. She pushed at one of them and it gave a little beneath her fingers.

An icy whisper ghosted the back of her neck, sending a wave of goose pimples up her spine. Lil pulled up sharp and then slowly turned round.

Nedly was standing behind her, at the top of the stairs, hands in pockets, looking miserable. 'I didn't mean to scare you.'

Lil's pulse was racing but she bit back on the jitters and gave him a reproving snort. 'You could give someone a heart attack with a stunt like that.'

'LIL!' Her mum shouted up the stairs again.

'COMING!' Lil yelled back and then lowered her voice again. 'That was some trick, Nedly.' She narrowed her eyes at him. 'How did you get out of there so quickly? And what were you doing in the airing cupboard in the first place. Have you been in there all night? How did you even fit?'

'Actually, it's bigger than it looks,' Nedly began. 'You see, there's this . . .'

Lil wasn't listening. She threw a jumper over her pyjama top and with a quick 'follow me'

set off down the landing. 'You know, you could have just said you didn't have anywhere else to go. You didn't have to go hide in a cupboard.'

Nedly attempted to interrupt from several paces behind as they hurried down the hall. 'I wasn't hiding; I was . . .'

'Ready?' Lil said.

'No . . . I – What for?'

'If you're going to stay here, I need to introduce you to my mum so we can find you somewhere better than the airing cupboard.'

Nedly skidded to a halt. 'What, now?' His face dropped. 'What if she can't . . . I mean, some people . . .' He faltered. 'What if she doesn't –'

'Like you? Why wouldn't she? I won't tell her about you breaking in and all that stuff, don't worry.' She held out her hand. As he reached to take it Lil felt an icy breeze play over her fingers. It was a strange sensation, like opening a freezer door. Without thinking she pulled away. 'Come on.'

As they crept down the hall Lil heard Waldo

going hell for leather around on his wheel. They opened the kitchen door and the sound was dwarfed by the shrill cry of the kettle, which was boiling itself dry on the stove top. Naomi Potkin stood staring distractedly into the refrigerator.

Lil turned off the hob and the noise died away. 'Kettle's boiled. Hungry?' she asked Nedly, picking up a couple of satsumas from a bowl on the side and offering him one.

He shook his head at it fearfully. 'I'm OK.'

'Starving,' said her mum, taking the satsuma from Lil and stuffing it in her pocket then swigging back a mouthful of tea.

'Mum,' said Lil. 'There's someone I want you to meet.'

'OK then.' Naomi pulled an egg box and a pat of butter out of the fridge and shivered. She closed the door and walked straight past Nedly to unhook a frying pan from the rack on the wall.

Lil gave him an apologetic shrug. 'His name is Nedly.'

'Great,' said Naomi, ignoring him. 'About last night . . .'

'Yeah,' said Lil, remembering suddenly why she had been at the bus station in the first place. 'I waited for you outside the cinema.'

'I had to work late . . .' Naomi started to explain.

'For almost an hour,' Lil continued.

'I'm sorry.' Naomi reached out a hand to tuck Lil's hair behind her ear but Lil stepped out of reach. 'You know, you've got so good at looking after yourself that sometimes I forget you still need looking after.'

'I don't need looking after,' Lil snorted. 'It's just that if someone says they are going to do something they should do it.'

'You're right. I am sorry.' Naomi pulled her daughter in for a hug and the scent of burnt matches hit Lil again.

'What *is* that smell?' she said, burying her nose in her mother's lapels.

'Oh, that.' Naomi quickly peeled off the jacket, balled it up and took a deep, analytical sniff. 'It's nothing.' She stuffed it in the washing machine.

'It doesn't smell like nothing,' Lil persevered.

'It's just a bit of burning fleece,' her mum admitted, turning back to the stove. She cracked the eggs into the pan and gave them a frantic stir.

'From . . . ?' Lil dropped two slices of bread into the toaster.

'There was an incident at work last night: a fire in the Mayor's Office. His sheepskin coat was the only thing I could find to damp the flames.'

Lil frowned. 'What were you doing in the Mayor's Office – I thought no one except the mayor and his bodyguard were allowed in there?'

Naomi paused mid-stir. 'I just had to pick up some routine files and things. It wasn't anything really, only a very little fire, and anyway the mayor was out cold the whole time. He probably wouldn't have even have known I was there.'

'So, how did it start?' Lil narrowed her eyes into the Penetrating Squint.

'Beats me.' Naomi seemed like she was immune to the Squint; all her attention seemed to be focused on scraping the burnt bits of egg off the bottom of the pan.

'But didn't anyone think it was strange that it was you who put the fire out? What about the bodyguard?'

'Look, no one was there to think anything and I didn't stick around,' Naomi said quickly. 'I had work to get on with so that was that.' She put down the spoon and took hold of Lil's chin firmly between her finger and thumb, tilting her head so they were eye to eye. 'It wasn't a big deal so just forget about it, OK?'

'Fine.' Lil shrugged and Naomi kissed her on the forehead. 'Anyway –' she looked from her mum to Nedly and then back again – 'aren't you going to say hello?'

Naomi pulled a slice of warm bread from the toaster and took a bite out of it. 'Look, love, I can't stay. I have to go back into work to help clear up the mess; there are papers and things that need to be sorted.' She took a pot down from a high shelf and pulled out a five-pound note. 'After breakfast why don't you get the bus into town? Go to the cinema or something.'

'Now? What about Nedly?'

'I'll meet him later.'

Nedly stood in the middle of the kitchen, his cheeks darkening as awkwardness turned into mortification. Lil was confused. 'But you're meeting him now.'

'Sorry, love, no time!' Naomi raced out of the kitchen, grabbing her rain mac off the hook in the hallway as she passed it.

'But it's Saturday . . . !' Lil yelled after her. The toast suddenly pinged as the front door slammed. Moments later they heard an exhaust splutter followed by a rubber squeal as the Datsun pulled away at speed.

Lil was dumbfounded. 'Sorry, Nedly. She's not normally that bad.'

Nedly looked relieved. 'It's OK.'

'It's not OK.' Bottles and jars rattled as she yanked open the fridge door and let it exhale icily in her face. 'She looked right through you –' Lil stared angrily into the dazzling white interior of the ice box – 'as if you weren't really there. Just like that idiot in the bus station. I don't know what's wrong with people in this town.' She turned slowly to face Nedly. His shoulders were curled inwards; his head hung down. The fridge light buzzed and went out.

'But I can see you – you're as real as me, right?' She poked out a finger to prod him in the chest but he took a step away. Lil frowned to herself as she laid the toast on a plate and spooned the eggs on top. 'Ketchup?'

He gazed hungrily at it. 'There's not enough for two. You have it.'

'We can share. Looks delicious, right?' Lil picked up a couple of forks and slid one across the table towards him. 'De-licious!' Nedly nodded and sat on his hands as though he was trying to stop them from doing something stupid. 'Come on,' said Lil. 'Tuck in.'

'No, thanks,' he said reluctantly. 'I'm fine.'

'Go on.' She pushed the plate towards him.

'I'll eat it later.' His leg started twisting restlessly.

'It will be cold by then.'

'Maybe I like it cold.'

'No one likes it cold.' Lil was beginning to get impatient. 'Just take it.' She held out the fork but Nedly backed away from the glinting prongs. He wasn't sweating, but he looked like he should have been. He pursed his lips and put his hands as far into his pockets as they would go. Lil put the cutlery back down on the table.

'You can't take it, can you?'

'Of course I can.'

'What's the matter with you?' she whispered.

'Nothing!' Nedly replied, a little too loudly. He turned to leave but finding the door closed he just walked up to it and stood there.

'Don't you want any breakfast then?'

He shook his head sadly.

'Not even a satsuma? Come on. I've got one each. Catch!' Lil threw it at Nedly.

He turned as it left her fingertips and reached out a hand to deflect it but missed. He shouted, 'No!' as the orange hit his stomach, disappeared through it, bounced on the lino, and rolled under the sideboard.

It took Lil's brain half a minute to take in what her eyes had just seen. As the second hand of the kitchen clock hammered its way through 180 degrees, she stared at Nedly with unblinking eyes; her jaw dropped a fraction of an inch and she held her last breath inside until she could swallow it. When she finally exhaled, her lips were still trembling.

Nedly was panic-stricken. He spluttered: 'That orange is going to go mouldy under there.'

'I know it will,' said Lil. 'But that's not the point. The point is you couldn't catch it, could you?'

'I could have if it hadn't been such a rubbish throw,' he said lamely.

Lil fired a raised eyebrow at him. 'Really? So

why don't you fetch it out from under there for me and I'll throw it again?'

He narrowed his eyes at her. 'I don't want to.'

'Nedly, the satsuma went right through you. It went through your belly and out the other side. You don't think there's anything weird about that?'

Nedly looked as though he was trying to think of an explanation.

'Don't try to think of an explanation. We both know why you couldn't catch it and it's time to face up to reality.'

'You must have thrown it pretty hard.'

'No I didn't. The satsuma went through you because you're not really there. So you must be a –' Lil could hardly believe what she was about to say. 'You're a ghost, Nedly.'

A look of abject horror struck Nedly. He gasped at her and then ran through the kitchen wall with a pop and vanished.

Lil shot out of the back door just in time to see him disappear through the garden wall; by the time she got to the alley beyond the back yard he was nowhere to be seen.

'Nedly? I'm sorry!' she called out. 'Are you there?' There was a cold patch to her left near to some bins. Lil turned to it. 'Nedly?'

She shivered as a curl of mist formed in the cold spot and coalesced into the outline of a boy, pale and wide-eyed. He sniffed miserably. 'That was a rubbish throw.'

'I'm sorry,' said Lil. 'You could have just told me.'

'Told you what?'

'Did you think I wouldn't notice?' Lil reached out to touch him but he flinched away; the tips of her finger just brushed his shoulder and sank through it. He felt light and cold like falling snow.

Nedly gave her a look of pure outrage and yelled: 'I am not a ghost – you can see me, you're talking to me. That means I'm real. That proves it!'

'But no one else can see you. Just me. Mum wasn't ignoring you. Neither was that man in

45

the bus station. They couldn't see you.' She looked him square in the eyes. 'You're a ghost, Nedly. Admit it.'

'I am not. You are . . .' He scowled at her and small grey patches appeared on his cheeks.

'That's the worst come-back in the books.'

'No it isn't.'

Lil folded her arms. 'You're right, *that* was. You're not really a Missing Persons case are you, Nedly?'

He shook his head sadly.

'If you're a ghost that means you're already d . . .' She faltered when she saw the stricken look on Nedly's face. 'It means you're de . . .'

The bin lids in the alley began to hum, and then rattle. Lil felt the vibrations of the approaching train thrumming in the concrete beneath her feet. She struggled to shout over the freight train. 'Look, Nedly, let's face it, it means that you're DEAD!' The last word rang out in the low chug and shunt that followed the train.

Nedly flickered like a hologram; Lil could see

the bricks of the alley wall appear through his sweatshirt. When he spoke his voice came out like a whisper so faint that it could have been the whistle of the wind. 'But I don't want to be dead.'

Lil felt a tear prick the back of her eye. She looked away, sniffed it back and cleared her throat.

'I know, Nedly. No one does but there it is. That's, you know, life. Now, I don't know much about ghosts – other than what I've read – but you're still walking the earth so for my money that means you're not currently at peace. It may be that you've come to a sticky end – had you thought of that?'

Nedly shrugged.

'In my book, an unquiet spirit means only one thing.' Lil fixed him with a steely glare. 'Murder.'

The word 'murder' hung in the air between them like a corpse from a gibbet.

Lil pushed it to one side. 'Come on, we've got work to do.'

Nedly peered at her from behind a lock of hair. 'Aren't you scared?'

Lil pulled the remaining satsuma out of her pocket and peeled it thoughtfully. 'Probably not as much as I should be.'

Chapter 5

Research

Lil and Nedly had the top deck of the City Bus all to themselves and they sat right at the front. A couple of people had tried to sit nearby but the strange atmosphere moved them downstairs again. The air around Lil was so cold that the mist on the window had frosted, the 'Stopping' sign kept blinking on and off at random, and the seats across the aisle creaked eerily as the bus swung round corners.

'First thing is,' said Lil, buttoning up her mac

against the chill, 'we have to find out who you are, I mean . . . were. Before. We need an I.D. Then we can see if there was anyone you knew who might have wanted to . . . harm you.'

Nedly shuddered.

'Sorry,' Lil winced. 'There's no easy way to say it.'

'So, where are we going?'

'We're going to search the Archives, Nedly, the secret store of articles that document the recent history of Peligan and its citizens. Not everyone has access but lucky for you, it's a place I'm pretty familiar with.' Lil tapped the side of her nose ominously. 'That's how I came to know about the *Chronicle*.'

'What's the *Chronicle*?'

She gave him an exasperated look. 'It used to be the main newspaper here, before the Mayor's Office closed it down and founded the *Herald*. Can you guess who the Chief Reporter was?' She didn't wait for an answer. 'A. J. McNair.'

'Who?'

'Don't you know anything?' With a furtive

glance over her shoulder to make sure they were still alone, she pulled a worn-looking paperback out of her rucksack. It was titled *McNair and the Free Press.*

'This is not just a biography,' she explained. 'It's *the* essential text for investigative reporters.' She flipped it over to show Nedly the information on the back.

He read aloud: 'Arthur James McNair was the chief investigative reporter for the *Chronicle*. The *Klaxon* was founded in his name after he vanished in mysterious circumstances during the election campaign for the previous mayor Al Davious's second term of office. Three days later McNair's body was dragged from the Kowpye River. It appeared that he had stumbled in there and drowned. This book tells the story of –'

'What it doesn't say there,' Lil interrupted, dropping her voice to a conspiratorial whisper, 'was that McNair disappeared when he was on the brink of exposing the scandal surrounding the elections. McNair had been asking Davious some very interesting questions about the misallocation of funds.

'After McNair disappeared the *Chronicle* was shut down. He never filed the story but it was picked up a few weeks later by an underground newspaper pamphlet and distributed anonymously and so the *Klaxon* was born.

'The *Klaxon* tells it the way it really is. It asks the questions we should all be asking.'

'McNair sounds like a good person.' Nedly nodded approvingly.

'He was,' said Lil quietly, touching the silhouette with her index finger. 'Maybe the last good person Peligan City will ever see. He really stood for something; he spoke out against all of this.' She lowered her voice even further and added darkly, 'And they killed him for it.'

'Who wrote the book?' Nedly asked her.

'A journalist calling herself "Marsha Quake" but that's an alias, I checked. It's really well researched,' Lil told him admiringly. 'She's probably his second biggest fan. After me,' she added. 'I would lend it to you but I have to keep it close because if anyone found out I had it, they would confiscate it and put me in jail.'

'Really?' Nedly was sceptical.

Lil flashed him a dare-devil look. 'Maybe. It's contraband because it's full of allegations of corruption against Peligan City's rich and influential, and no one is allowed to say that stuff in public any more.'

'Cool,' said Nedly, obviously impressed. 'Where did you get your copy?'

'I borrowed it.' Lil gave him a sly wink.

The corner of a black-and-white photo was poking out like a shark's fin from between the pages. Nedly spied it. 'What's that?'

Lil reluctantly pulled out the photo and held it up for Nedly. 'It's just an old picture I found. I use it as a bookmark.'

'Is that your mum?'

Lil nodded.

'You really take after her,' Nedly said.

'So they tell me,' Lil muttered through gritted teeth. She untucked her hair and flattened it over her ears.

'It's not just the ears,' Nedly explained. 'Anyway, it was supposed to be a compliment.' He peered closer at the man beside her. 'Is that your dad?'

Lil shrugged. 'No. He was just some old boyfriend, I suppose. I don't know who any of the other people are. Mum doesn't like to talk about it. It doesn't matter anyway. If I have dad he's not around.'

'Do you miss him?'

'Never knew the guy – what's to miss?' Lil leant her forehead against the damp glass of the window and gazed out at the rain. 'I'm not complaining. It's tough all over. I'll bet you miss your folks, Nedly.'

He didn't reply straight away, and when he did his voice sounded like it had shrunk. 'I don't remember them.'

'It will come back.' Lil tried for upbeat and optimistic. 'You just need your memory jogged.'

Nedly smiled shyly at her and said, 'You know, I was invisible until I met you.'

'I'm pretty sure you're still invisible, Nedly. I don't know why it is that I can see you, but you should prepare yourself; I might be the only one who can.'

'I know,' he agreed. 'But the way I see it, I got pretty lucky there, didn't I, with you turning out to be an investigative reporter. A normal person might not have been able to . . . you know . . . solve the case. But I knew you would help, as soon as I saw you take that kid's poster at the bus station. I knew the poster was significant.'

'Well,' Lil said uncertainly, 'I'll give it my best shot.'

Nedly's eyes shone. 'I know you will, Lil. I bet on it.'

Lil gave him what she hoped was a confident nod before turning her face away, so she could bite her lip while pretending to watch the grey city slide past.

They got off at the last stop before the city centre. As soon as her feet hit the pavement Lil set off with a purposeful walk. Nedly had to jog to catch her up.

'We need to run a couple of searches, find out who you are . . . might take a bit of digging . . .'

They crossed a road and passed a row of shops. The streets of Peligan were littered with discount stores, credit exchanges, betting shops and laundrettes, but the old city still haunted the new, if you knew where to look. Faded signs painted on the brickwork suggested there had once been a flower shop, a deli and a baker's but now metal graffiti-covered shutters had been pulled down over the windows and padlocked to the pavement. Some of the doors had metal grilles across them, and although the signs said 'Open' it wasn't clear what they were selling.

'. . . We'll start with the facts. We have a name . . . sort of. Let's see if you made the papers.'

'But we don't even know – Lil?' Nedly suddenly found himself walking alone. 'Lil?'

He back-tracked a few paces and found an alleyway, which branched off to the left. He followed until it opened up into a courtyard. Black metal fire escapes zigzagged down at the backs of the buildings that surrounded the flagstones. Lil was in the corner wobbling around on an upturned bottle crate, while reaching up to a small window that was slightly ajar. She put one foot against the wall, bent her rubber sole to the brick and jumped, grabbing the window ledge and hauling herself upwards. Crouching on the ledge she reached inside and unhooked the window. It swung inwards and Lil followed it.

Nedly watched her slide out of sight.

'What are you doing?' he called after her.

Lil reappeared in the window. 'Come on! Before someone sees you.'

Nedly didn't move. After a few seconds Lil stuck her head back through, not realising what she had said until she saw the look on his face.

'Sorry, I forgot. Come on!'

On the other side of the window was a toilet cubicle. Nedly dropped silently onto the loo seat and stepped down. Lil was waiting by the hand basins, dusting some flakes of paint from the window frame off her clothes.

'Did we just break in?'

'The window was open,' Lil said by way of an answer. 'You know you should take it as a compliment – that I forgot you were . . . you know . . . not really there.' Nedly winced. 'I mean, invisible.' Lil pulled open the exit door, cursing herself under her breath.

They walked into an oval atrium. Above them a round window threw a cylinder of dusty light down to the marble floor. The curved walls were hung with posters advertising citizenship meetings, all tattered and yellowed with age. They flapped in the draught that came from under the big main doors that were locked shut with a plank nailed across them.

'Where are we?' asked Nedly.

Lil waded through the drifts of dead leaves and junk mail that were banked up against the walls and picked up a book from the heap beneath the letter box. She turned the first couple of pages and then held it out for Nedly to see. The stamp read 'Property of Peligan City Library'.

'I didn't even know we had a library,' said Nedly.

Lil peeled off a piece of old sticky tack and paper that had been left stuck to the wall when a notice had been torn down. She pointed at the corresponding 'Save our Library' poster that was still lying on the floor beneath it. 'Not many people do,' she said. 'Officially Mayor Dean closed it during his first term in office, just after he shut down all the high schools. Probably he didn't want people getting too clever and finding out about what was going on.'

Lil pressed a four-digit code into a keypad at the side of a sturdy door that was signposted 'Reading Room'. They heard a buzz and some metallic clunking and the door swung open.

Inside it was a different world. The ceiling was domed and decorated with ornate white plaster. The walls were lined with books; tall, dark wooden shelves reached up to a mezzanine, which encircled the room. Free-standing shelves radiated like wheel spokes, forming corridors to the centre in which stood six polished desks, each with a green glass-hooded reading light.

Nedly was wide-eyed.

Lil winked at him and then whispered, 'It has to be a secret: the mayor would close it down all over again if he knew it was still open.'

'So how come you know about it?'

'My mum used to bring me here when I was small. I used to look at the newspapers and things while she did her library business.'

'What's "library business"?'

'I don't know, returning books and stuff.'

'Before it was closed?'

'Yeah, of course. And then one day we just stopped coming and that must have been when they shut it down. So then I found my own way back in.'

'How did you know the special code?'

Lil gave him the Squint. 'Why all the questions?'

'I don't know.' Nedly shrugged defensively. 'I've just never been in a library before.' He scanned the shelves of maps and atlases. 'So, who looks after all this? Arghhh!'

A tall woman with very short grey hair and green-framed glasses suddenly appeared from behind a shelf and walked through Nedly with a shiver. She was followed by a black cat, which slunk out from between a gap in the bookshelves.

The cat took one look at Nedly, pinned back its ears and hissed.

Nedly looked uncomfortable. 'Go away!' he hissed back, stepping behind Lil and peering over her shoulder.

The cat bared its fangs and its eyes bulged.

Lil nodded at it in a way that meant: *What's up with Milton?*

The librarian shrugged as if to say: *He's a cat – who knows?* She raised a questioning eyebrow at Lil and held out her hand.

Lil took out her notebook. She tore out a page and carefully wrote 'Missing Boy' on it and passed it the librarian, who looked at it and frowned. She took it to a stack of small cardboard drawers, each labelled alphabetically, and opened the one that said 'M'. She flicked through the yellowed index cards and pulled one out. Taking it with her to the lift at the back of the room, she pulled the metal grille aside and pushed a button. With a clunk and squeal the elevator came to life and the librarian was slowly lowered out of sight.

Nedly whispered, 'You aren't allowed to talk in here?'

Lil shrugged. 'Who knows. It's usually just me and Logan here and she's deaf, so we just got used to not talking, I suppose. She likes things written down anyway – for accuracy.'

Ten minutes later the squeaking, reeling sound of the lift started up again and the librarian returned with a stack of newspapers. She carried them over to one of the desks and turned on the lamp.

Lil gave Logan a look that said: *We have to look through all of these?*

The librarian nodded and left them to it.

Chapter 6

The Scourge of the Underworld

They focused on a newspaper each. Lil spread them out on the desk and turned on the green glass lamp; it buzzed and grew dim whenever Nedly moved near it until Lil hissed at him to 'Keep still!'

They worked in silence apart from Nedly's repeated requests for Lil to turn the pages. After a few minutes she lost her temper.

'Look, it's taking twice as long to find the articles because I have to keep turning the pages for you as well as my own!'

'I'm *trying* to help.'

'I know, but . . . Forget it.' She turned the next page and started scanning it, then stopped and looked up at him. 'It's just occurred to me, Nedly –' she swivelled round to face him – 'that you're sitting on that chair.'

'I know.'

Lil raised her eyebrows. 'So you can't turn a page or pick up a satsuma, but you can sit on a chair? That doesn't make any sense.'

Nedly was horrified. He stared at his legs with dread as though he was about to see them sink through the wooden seat.

Nothing happened.

'You shouldn't be able to do that. It's the same as walking on a pavement or up stairs; if you can't touch an object then you shouldn't be able to do any of it.'

Nedly gulped; he looked like he was trying not to panic. 'What are you saying?'

Lil looked pleased. 'I'm saying you *can* catch a satsuma and you can also turn the pages. Maybe you just have to concentrate more, or maybe there's some kind of knack to it. I don't know, but the fact is – it's possible. You should at least try.'

She had to hand it to him, Nedly really did try. The table rattled, and his chair fell over. Lil sat through a series of crashing and straining sounds as he attempted to force the pages to turn. He flapped his hands at them, blew at the edges, windmilled his arms, he even commanded them to turn in a low and terrible voice. If anyone but Lil had heard him they would have come running to see what the commotion was but no one could, so Lil sat there, apparently alone in the study area, stewing in an irritable silence with her fingers jammed in her ears and a permanent grimace, until finally she had enough.

'OK, OK! she yelled. 'Forget it!'

For a few moments the only sound in the library was Lil's angry breathing, and then they heard a rattle of footsteps. Lil jumped up to peer round the shelves but whoever it was had vanished, leaving the door to the librarian's office swinging shut. Logan was still sitting at her desk marking up some documents.

Lil sat back down thoughtfully and murmured. 'That's always happening in here and I never see who it is.'

Nedly shouted in frustration, 'I've tried everything!'

The mystery of the unknown occupant of the Librarian's Office had distracted Lil enough for her temper to die down. 'Don't worry about it,' she whispered. 'I'll turn the pages; it's no big deal.'

'It's a big deal to me.' Nedly slammed a white-knuckled fist on the desk. Lil noticed that the scratch on the back of his hand, the raised white line with a thin blood-beaded centre, hadn't even begun to heal yet.

Lil nodded at the clenched fist. 'You shouldn't have been able to do that either.'

As Nedly glared at her and then at the inanimate paper. One of the pages began to curl up, as though lifted by a breeze. Lil held her breath. Nedly bored his unblinking eyes into the pages with a look of complete determination, until they began to twitch with the effort. Lil was about to advise him to give up before his eyeballs burst when, all of a sudden, it happened. In a flurry of newsprint the pages fluttered over in quick succession, like a sprung deck of cards.

'Not bad!' she said.

Nedly's eyes shone, but he shrugged modestly and said, 'It was too fast to actually read anything.'

'But it's a start.'

Lil smiled to herself. She thought there was probably a whole lot that Nedly could do, if he could work out how. She didn't even comment on how annoying the intermittent rustling sound was as Nedly practised rifling the pages, reading each spread in random order depending on where the paper opened.

After almost an hour of searching the *Herald* for the missing person report Lil noticed that Nedly was no longer turning the pages and had fallen silent. The air in the room had turned icy and the shadows cast from the desk lamp started to loom.

'You've found it then?' she whispered.

The article was small and near the back.

Concern for Missing Boy

Ten-year-old orphan Ned Stubbs was reported missing from the Hawks Memorial Orphanage last Tuesday morning. Despite the assurances of the local police force, the orphanage caretaker, Mr Emil Kolchak, told the Herald *yesterday that he did not believe that Stubbs would have run away and is concerned for his welfare. They have engaged local Private Investigator Absolom 'Abe' Mandrel to find the boy. Citizens with any information as to his whereabouts should contact Mandrel at his offices on Wilderness Lane.*

There was a blurred picture of Ned Stubbs. It must have been a school portrait as he was wearing a tie, a V-neck jumper and a forced smile.

Lil watched Nedly's eyes move back and forth across the page as he read through the text over and over again. Finally they settled on the photograph. He reached out a finger to touch it, but it slipped through the paper, and he drew back sadly. 'It says here I'm an orphan.' His mouth turned down. 'At least no one missed me.'

Lil looked at the date. 'You've been . . . you know what . . . for a whole year already.' She watched Nedly trying to blink back the tears that had welled up under his eyelids. 'It must be a bit of a shock, right, seeing it there in black and white?' She tried to put a comforting arm round his shoulders but whipped it away again when it dropped through his back, jolting her with an icy shudder. Nedly didn't seem to notice. His pale face had turned white and filmy; his shoulders curled in, making him look even thinner.

'I bet they missed you at the orphanage, Nedly. They hired this Mandrel guy, didn't they?'

'Yeah. A year ago.' He got to his feet. Three of the four globe lightshades that hung down from the ceiling pinged and went out. He swallowed hard. 'I can't do this. I don't want to know. I need to get out of here. I need some . . . air . . . or something.' Nedly started skirting the walls looking for an open door.

Lil called quietly after him. 'Wait for me outside. I'm going to check out this detective.'

She watched Nedly give up trying to find an exit and disappear through a bookshelf. A row of box files fell off in his wake, one after the other like synchronised swimmers. Logan appeared round the bookshelf, frowning, and Lil quickly scribbled the name 'Absolom "Abe" Mandrel' on a fresh page in her notebook, tore it out and handed it to her before she had a chance to start tidying the box files away.

A short while later, the librarian carried over a thin pile of newspapers and placed them on Lil's desk with the index card.

Lil laid them out in front of her, sharpened her pencil and started taking notes.

The first and oldest article was from the *Chronicle* and mentioned a Detective Constable Mandrel who had single-handedly busted an illegal bootleg operation in a downtown warehouse and had received an award for Outstanding Service to the Police Force. The next two articles were dated five years on and just name-checked him as part of the Serious and Organised Crime Squad (SOCS) that had infiltrated and then brought down a rare-diamond smuggling ring and then, two years later, a protection racket based out of the Lick and Spittle Boxing Club.

The biggest story was a double-page spread from an early edition of the *Herald*. Mandrel had been in charge of a large-scale operation that had led to the capture of the notorious Lucan Road Mob. The ringleader, mob boss and extortionist Ramon LeTeef, his associate, renegade scientist and inventor Dr C. Gallows, and their assorted henchmen had been arrested on numerous charges, which included theft, embezzlement, fraud, kidnap, violent assault, blackmail, armed robbery and two counts of attempted murder.

Under the subheading 'Scourge of the

Underworld' there was a picture of Detective Mandrel in his police-issue trench coat, his trilby pulled down and shading one eye. His wide jaw was set in grim determination, his glare was steely, and there was, Lil noticed, the slight suggestion of a shadow under his eyes. She looked closely at the face of the man in the picture and then slowly reached into her rucksack and pulled out her copy of *McNair and the Free Press*, flicking through the pages until she found the photograph of her mother.

As she held it up against the grainy newsprint image of the detective her heartbeat started to thrum like a double-bass solo. One man had a twinkle in his eye and a lopsided grin, the other was grave-faced and almost scowling, but there was no doubt in her mind that it was the same man, and that for whatever reason and albeit many years ago, this great detective was someone her mother had once known – which made him practically a friend of the family.

She licked her fingers and turned to the last article. It was a front-page story. Lil read it through quickly.

Is this Justice?

The trial of the deranged mastermind behind the Lucan Road Mob's most startling crimes was concluded at Peligan City Courthouse yesterday.

Dr C. Gallows was found to be criminally insane and will be committed to Rorschach Asylum for the indefinite future. On account of his testimony against the doctor and other notable henchmen, former mob boss Ramon LeTeef has been granted impunity from criminal prosecution.

When asked what he thought of the outcome of the trial, Detective Absolom 'Abe' Mandrel, who was in charge of the original investigation, made no comment.

There was a picture of Mandrel leaving the courthouse, one hand up to block a camera, the other arm in a sling.

Lil swung her chair back on two legs and chewed thoughtfully on the end of her pencil. 'Sounds like a stitch-up,' she said to the photograph. 'You must have been fuming.' She looked at the date on the paper. It was published more than twelve years ago. There was no mention of Mandrel in the papers from that entry until the Missing Boy article. *So where had he been all that time?*

Pondering this thought, Lil tore out one final page before closing her notebook, wrote two words on it and then heaved both piles of newspapers into her arms and carried them back to the desk.

She handed the paper to Logan and waited. *Last one.*

Lil was almost ready to give up by the time the librarian appeared behind her, her green spectacles only just visible above the pile of newspapers she was carrying. They were all the

Herald and behind her was a trolley loaded with more editions.

Lil looked at the pile in a way that said, *All of these?*

Logan put a copy of the paper on the desk and flicked through to the last pages. She reached the personal ads and ran a finger down the page until she found what she was looking for. Lil quickly read the ad. She looked over at the piles and raised her eyebrows in a way that meant: 'Is there one of these in all of those?'

Logan nodded.

Lil smiled a *Thanks* and got to her feet.

Nedly was sitting on the back of a bench opposite the library staring up at the dirty grey stone columns stained a murky green with exhaust fumes and algae. On the roof stood four figures, the old gods of learning, philosophy, truth and wisdom, looking balefully down on the city as their limbs crumbled away. The large leaded windows were boarded up and covered in graffiti. Amongst all the tags and obscene sketches Nedly picked out a phrase in red spray-painted letters. It read '*Ipsa scientia potestas est*', and the trademark tag of a 'K' in a circle. It was the same 'K' as was on the cover of the *Klaxon.*

Lil hopped up to sit beside him. 'It means "Knowledge itself is power".' Nedly didn't look as impressed as she'd hoped. 'It's a saying. In Latin. Which is an old language no one speaks any more,' she added.

'I know what Latin is,' Nedly grumbled; still slumped on the bench, chin in his hands and shoulders sagging.

'Cheer up,' said Lil. 'I've got some amazing news!'

Nedly stared down at his shoelaces and sighed. 'What?'

'That private investigator, Mandrel, the one who's been looking for you –'

'The one that didn't find me.'

'The one that hasn't found you *yet*. Well, I know him already – sort of. I mean, he's an old friend of Mum's.' She pulled the picture from her pocket and jabbed a finger at the trilby-hatted man. 'This is him, right there.'

'You said he was a nobody.'

'Well, it turns out he's a somebody – a famous detective!'

'Great.' Nedly sighed again.

'You don't sound so thrilled.'

'No, I am. It's really great,' Nedly said, not sounding any more thrilled than before.

Lil's eyes were shining. 'We should meet him, as soon as possible. I mean, you know, to find out about your case. I reckon we can solve this thing in no time with the three of us working together.'

'I hope so.'

'Oh, I nearly forgot. I have something to show you.'

Beside the bench was a litter bin; inside were the remains of the morning's paper that had been soaking up the grease from a chip wrapping. Lil picked it out and turned to the second-to-last page. She held it up for Nedly to see and pointed to the advert.

Appeal for Missing Boy
Please help. Do you have information relating to the disappearance of Ned Stubbs? Reply to the Hawks Memorial Orphanage, Bun Hill, Peligan City West.

Nedly didn't look at her. 'So? They put out an advert. Big deal.'

'Not just one – there are hundreds in there. Someone at the orphanage has put that advert in the *Herald* every day for the last year. You should have seen the pile.'

Nedly squinted up at her. 'Really?'

'Yes, really. So someone cares what happens to you, a lot. And they're not the only one, so . . .'

Nedly shrugged despondently.

Lil jumped down off the bench and turned to face him. 'Look, I know you've had . . . a bad time lately and you probably think you've got nothing to . . .' She faltered. '. . . go on for . . . but a whole year has gone by and not even this Mandrel guy could find you. Whoever did this probably thinks they've got away with it. So we've got to solve this, Nedly; we've got to prove them wrong!'

The silence that followed Lil's speech was broken only by the wheels of a tramp's trolley as an old woman passed between them.

Lil softened her voice. 'I know you're worried, Nedly, but I won't let you down.'

After a couple of long seconds he cracked a begrudging smile. 'OK. What's first?'

'First, we better hook up with Mandrel and find out what he knows. Believe me, Nedly, with him on the case, you've got nothing to worry about – he's the business.'

There was a well-thumbed directory in a nearby phone box. Lil flicked through to the right section and ran her finger down the page until she found it.

'Mandrel, Absolom. There's an address on Shoe Street – wait, there's more below it. Absolom Mandrel Private Investigations, 154c Wilderness Lane. OK, let's go! I've got a good feeling about this, Nedly.'

Chapter 7

154c Wilderness Lane

Lil's 'good feeling' took a knock early that afternoon when they arrived at Wilderness Lane. The street was lined with derelict buildings that had once been respectable. The decorative plasterwork was crumbling, the glass orbs of the cast-iron lamp-posts were algae-stained, and the pavement was cracked beyond repair. Sirens wailed in the background and the low solitary song of a saxophone spiralled up from one of the dark basement clubs. It wasn't exactly the business district Lil had imagined. The only business she could see, apart from a betting shop and a pawnbroker's was a fold-away table manned by two boys trying to sell things out of a suitcase.

Lil found number 154 and paused as she reached for the buzzer for C. She took a deep breath and focused on the silhouette of McNair in her mind's eye as she got her act together. *Play it cool, gather evidence, establish the facts.* 'OK,' she said in a low voice, instinctively glancing over her shoulder to make sure no one was in earshot. 'Mandrel won't be able to see you, Nedly, so I'll do all the talking, OK? And I'll have to pretend you're not there either or else he'll think I'm crazy.'

Nedly looked hurt.

'But it's important that you are there, OK? I might need backup.'

Lil hit the buzzer, and said 'Hello' into the intercom. There was no reply.

Nedly looked nervously up the street. 'Maybe he's out?'

'Maybe,' said Lil. She pushed at each of the buzzers in turn.

'Let's just go,' muttered Nedly. He was hopping nervously from foot to foot.

Lil pursed her lips. 'The fact is, we're looking for a very dangerous criminal, Nedly. A child-killer, so we could do with some help – someone who knows how to bust a few heads. Someone like Mandrel.' She buzzed again, holding all the buttons down with the palm of her hand for several seconds.

Finally a throaty voice that sounded like it had just been woken from a late-afternoon stupor yelled: 'What?'

'Pizza delivery,' said Lil cheerfully. 'One large pizza, extra garlic bread, special promotion.'

With a click the door opened.

The building smelt of damp. There were orange-coloured water marks spreading across the ceiling, which bulged in places. The vinyl wallpaper in the hallway looked like it was sweating and the brown felt carpet had worn to nothing on the stairs. Nedly peered at the naked bulb that swung overhead. A dewdrop of water hung from it and then fell through him onto a darkened rug that was covering up some rotten-looking floorboards.

'This place is a death trap,' he muttered, following Lil up the staircase.

On the third-floor landing was a door with a frosted-glass pane. The window read 'Absolom Mandrel Private Investigator' in flaking gold lettering.

Lil knocked on the glass and waited impatiently. There was no answer. She put an eye to the key hole and looked in. The shutters were down and she could only make out a bit of the floor in the dim rectangle of light that shone in through the door, but she could see that it was strewn with scraps of cardboard and scrunched-up pieces of paper and looked like it could do with a really good sweep.

She called out 'Mr Mandrel? Are you in? Hello? We have some information you might be interested in, regarding the disappearance of Nedly – Ned Stubbs.

'I told you he's not there,' said Nedly, anxiously checking the stairwell.

Lil pondered. 'Maybe we should wait inside?'

'It's locked.'

'We've come this far.' She appraised the door lock. 'I saw this once, in a film,' she said and took out her penknife. Sticking the blade between the door and the frame she started wiggling it.

Nedly looked nervously over his shoulder. 'You can't just break in to someone's office! What if he comes back?

'He'll never know we were here. I'll just take a quick poke around and then we'll come back another time.'

Lil levered the knife back and forth and up and down, not exactly sure what she was doing. 'Almost got it,' she said hopefully. 'Just a couple more turns.' With a creak and a snap, the wood on the door frame splintered and the door popped open.

'Open sesame!' she said with a flourish

'You've broken his door,' Nedly said accusingly. 'I think he will notice.'

Lil flung the door wide and a huddle of empty whisky bottles toppled over with a clatter, like pins at a bowling alley. She switched the light on and her heart lurched. 'Maybe not.'

The room was bare except for a large wooden desk covered in sticky rings where drinks had been spilt, an old, dented filing cabinet, and a coat stand that had been knocked over and left to lie there.

Nedly peered over the banister of the stairwell to check if anyone had been disturbed by the noise. He turned back to give Lil the all-clear but she was already in the office rifling through the filing cabinet.

'It's just empty folders,' she said, disappointed. She picked up the phone receiver. The line was dead. 'Mandrel is long gone.'

White spots dotted the yellowing walls where pictures had once been stuck and then ripped down again. The only things left up were a framed certificate that stated that A. Mandrel had passed his detective exams with distinction, and a graduation portrait of the young police recruit looking hopeful. It hung lopsided and the glass was cracked.

Lil stared at it long and hard. She saw her own reflection in the glass, and tried to mirror the set of his steely jaw.

'What are you looking at?' Nedly peered over her shoulder, close enough to make her shiver, and then a sound distracted them: the heavy creak of someone moving softly up the stairs.

Nedly darted out onto the landing and saw the shadow of a man rounding the stairwell, keeping close to the wall. He saw it raise one hand.

'Someone's coming. Hide!'

Lil looked around; there was nowhere to hide. She quickly turned off the lights, closed the door and then flattened herself to the wall beside it.

The shadow loomed across the frosted glass, engulfing the lettering. The door swung open, nearly hitting Lil in the face.

As the man in the doorway reached inside

for the light switch Lil panicked and slammed the door back shut, trapping his hand. The man cried out in surprise but he didn't withdraw his hand. Lil slammed it again, more forcefully. The hand fell to the floor. This time it was Lil's turn to cry out – the hand lay there at her feet, lifeless. Lil kicked it away from her and stood in front of the door trying to hold it closed while the man whose hand she had just severed tried to force it open.

'Argh! Help!' Lil squealed. 'I've got his hand! He's going to kill me.'

Nedly cast a cautious glance at the door and crept over to the hand. He peered at it.

The man outside had stopped rattling the door and fallen silent but they could still see his shadow. It looked like it was holding up a pair of pliers.

Lil gasped. She gave Nedly a look that said: *We have to get out of here!*

'Lil,' said Nedly. 'I think that's . . .'

From the hallway a gruff voice said 'I'm going

to open this door, nice and slow, and nobody moves, OK?'

Lil couldn't have moved if she tried. Her eyes went to the shadow, to the hand, to Nedly, to the window. The door swung open and the man wielding the pliers stood there.

He had the same broad shoulders and cleft chin as the police officer in the photograph, but that was where the similarity ended. Absolom Mandrel was grizzled and overweight. His eyes were red-rimmed. He had several days' stubble growing on his chin and some kind of greasy egg stain on his rumpled shirt. His mac looked like it had once belonged to a tramp, and the rim of his hat was frayed.

He bent down and picked up the hand and screwed it on over the pliers. Lil looked at him, mystified.

'It's a prosthetic,' he said.

'What's that Swiss Army . . . thing?' Lil whispered.

Mandrel pulled off the rubber hand again

and opened and closed the crocodile mouth of the pliers. 'The hand is just for looks – the Swiss Army thing, as you call it, is a multifunctional device I adapted myself to get things done. This one is my driving attachment.' He mimicked steering the wheel and changing gear. 'Now, do you mind telling me what you're doing?'

'I – I . . .' Lil couldn't find the words. *Was this really the man in the photograph?* 'I thought you'd gone.'

'So you thought you'd just break in and have a poke around, eh?'

Lil shook the question off; she had a more pressing one. 'What happened to you?'

Mandrel looked down at his prosthetic hand. 'I lost it trying to apprehend a criminal.'

'I didn't mean that,' Lil explained slowly. She went over to the portrait and pointed an accusing finger at it. 'I mean, what happened to *you*?'

Mandrel pulled a hipflask out of his pocket, took a swig and then wiped his mouth on his sleeve. 'Mind your own beeswax, Wing Nut.'

He frowned at the splintered door frame and then gave her a hard look, which softened suddenly. 'Say, you look familiar; do I know you from somewhere?'

'No,' Lil replied quickly.

'Show him the photo!' urged Nedly.

'No!' Lil repeated.

'All right, I heard you the first time.' Mandrel narrowed his eyes at her. 'There's something about you, kid, reminds me of someone. Can't put my finger on it.' He shrugged and went over to the desk, opening all the drawers one by one, locating a half-empty bottle in the last one and stowing it away in his mac pocket. 'So what is your business here?'

Lil looked over at Nedly, who was staring glumly at Mandrel, disappointment all over his face. She knew just how he felt. 'Detective Mandrel, I have some information about one of your cases.'

Mandrel rubbed his eyes with a finger and thumb. 'I'm only working one case now and I sincerely doubt you know anything that could help me with that.'

'It's about Ned Stubbs. The Missing Boy.'

'Who?' He frowned at the naked bulb that hung from the ceiling as it buzzed and dimmed.

'The caretaker at the Hawks Memorial Orphanage hired you to find him. Last year.'

Abe looked confused for a moment. He took off his hat, wiped back his grizzled hair, and then replaced it. 'I remember. That case went cold.'

Chapter 8

On the Tail of Mandrel P.I.

'If he thinks he's off the hook, then he's got another think coming.' Lil scowled across the road at the windows of 154c Wilderness Lane from between the railings of a cellar stairwell. Only her eyes and the hood of her yellow mac were visible at the edge of the pavement.

Nedly was standing at street level in front of the railings. He looked down at her sadly. 'You're disappointed.'

A man in a crumpled suit hurried past,

splashing Lil in the face with dirty puddle water. 'Bleurgh!' Lil spluttered. 'Aren't you?'

'So why are we still here?'

'Because,' said Lil, rubbing the grime off her cheeks with her sleeve, 'Mandrel took your case and he's got no right to close it until it's solved.'

'He kicked us out, Lil.' The street lamp overhead flickered and dimmed. 'Well, he kicked you out. He's not interested in finding out what happened to me.'

'Well, he better get interested,' said Lil. 'Because I'm not going away.'

Lil had seen, and tasted, more than her fill of Wilderness Lane by 4 p.m., when the lights finally went out in the office of Absolom Mandrel P.I. After a few minutes the front door opened and the detective stepped out. They watched him turn down a side street and out of view.

'Right, let's follow him!' Lil hurried up the steps and across the road, flattening herself against a wall at the mouth of the lane. She stuck her head round the corner to see Mandrel's hulking silhouette blend into the shadows at the far end, waited until the sound of footsteps stomping through puddles had faded, and then gave Nedly the nod and they set off in pursuit.

They emerged onto a narrow lane bordered with thin rickety buildings that leant inwards, almost blocking out the sky. Mandrel walked doggedly, collar up, hat pulled down low, shouldering aside the rain, and anyone else who got in his way. It must have been some instinct, or maybe a gumshoe's old habits, that made him keep glancing over his shoulder as he moved through the huddles of people.

Lil dodged and weaved along behind him, cutting through the steam that rose up from the drains and took on the pink and blue neon glow of the shop signs. They were heading east, into the labyrinth of pawnshops and laundrettes, late-night grocery shops and takeaways.

Lil struggled to keep Mandrel in sight while

Nedly ran in her wake, trying and failing to avoid the passers-by who bustled Lil but pushed straight through him. The odd person shivered, but most were too wrapped up in their own business to mind the chilling sensation that followed.

They reached a crossroads and Lil shrank into the doorway of a boarded-up old hairdresser's, watching as the detective paused at a newsstand to buy a paper. Despite the rain he opened it up fully and seemed to be scanning the centre pages.

'He's not reading it,' whispered Nedly. 'He's looking over here.'

Lil waited in the shadows for him to make his move. 'Is he still looking?'

'Yes.'

'How about now?'

'Yes. I'll tell you when he does something else.'

A rough-sleeper who was propped up against the door in a muddle of bags and cardboard boxes coughed impatiently. He didn't worry

Lil. Sure, she was hiding in a doorway, whispering to an invisible associate, but in Peligan City plenty of people talked to themselves and no one paid them any attention. They kept to their own business and turned a blind eye to everything else.

'OK,' said Nedly. 'He's folding the paper, and tucking it under his arm. Now he's turning and walking towards . . .'

Lil poked her head out to watch Mandrel disappear into a doorway. The sign across the front window read 'Kam Moon Special Noodle Bar' in gold lettering and below it stretched a red and green Chinese dragon. The window was steamed up and all Lil could make out was the blue glow of an electric fly trap and the shadows of some plastic ferns.

'Shall we go in after him?' suggested Nedly.

'He'll see us.'

'He might see you,' Nedly pointed out with a grin.

'Good point. OK, you do it.'

He crossed the road and then, as soon as

someone opened the door to leave, he slipped inside.

Lil waited anxiously as the minutes passed. Neither Nedly nor Detective Mandrel emerged. No one did. She began to worry. What if it wasn't a noodle bar at all – what if it was a trap and Nedly had just walked right into it?

She was going to have to go after him. Lil took a deep breath, nipped through the traffic and opened the door.

'Phew!' said Nedly. 'I thought no one was ever going to open the door again.'

'You've just been standing on the other side of the door waiting for someone to open it?' Nedly blinked back at her. 'While I've been waiting out here in the rain for you to come out?'

Nedly frowned. 'You don't know what it's like passing through solid objects – it's not a good feeling.'

'Right,' said Lil irritably. 'Fine. Whatever. Where is the detective?'

'He's gone.'

'What! Impossible! Did you check the back way?'

'There wasn't one.'

'Nedly,' she said wearily. 'There's always a back way. He's given us the slip.'

Lil went up to the counter of the noodle bar and, fixing her face with an earnest smile, she asked the chef if he knew the detective that had just been in.

'Number twenty-four,' said the chef. 'Singapore-style noodles with spring roll.'

'I mean, do you know where he lives?'

The chef pointed his index finger up in the air and Lil followed it up to the ceiling. 'Right. Thanks.'

She went back outside and looked up. There, above the Kam Moon Special Noodle Bar, was the shabbiest-looking hotel she had ever seen.

Chapter 9

The Mingo

The sign for the Flamingo Hotel had been broken for so long that no one could remember its real name. To Peligan City it was just 'The Mingo', a two-bit dive for end-of-the-roaders. The luminous tubing outline of a bowing flamingo see-sawed over a dark stairwell. A red 'Vacancies' sign buzzed on and off in the front window.

An oily-looking man in a raincoat staggered out of the front door with a doll-faced woman on his arm, and left it swinging. Lil ran across the street and slipped in before it clicked shut; Nedly wasn't so lucky. The door closed through him with a sucking noise. He stood in the hallway shivering and looking queasy.

Lil ducked behind a deflated settee in the old reception lobby just in time to see Mandrel standing on the first-floor landing in front of a wall of pigeon holes. The brown-paper bag containing his takeaway noodles was tucked under his arm. She watched him check through the stack of mail, extract a few envelopes and flyers and then return the rest. Then he pushed the button at the bottom of the stairwell that turned on the lights and wearily began climbing the steps.

Lil listened to his footsteps growing fainter, then the lights went off and a few seconds later a second set came on further up the stairs.

'OK,' she whispered. 'Let's go.'

She scanned the pigeon holes until she found the one labelled 'Mandrel. 7.3 Hawaiian Island Suite'. Lil noted he had a flyer for the Black

Pug Eatery – she checked inside for a copy of the *Klaxon*, but it was empty.

'Seven-three,' said Nedly. 'Is that the seventh floor?'

They looked over at the lift where an 'Out of Order' sign was hung across the metal grille, fencing off what appeared to be an empty shaft, and then upwards at the multitude of staircases that zigzagged between landings, and sighed.

Every light seemed to be timed to go off shortly before the next button could be pressed so in between floors Lil found herself alternately recoiling from the grubby palm-tree-print wallpaper that was smeared with something she hoped was soy sauce and then plunged into darkness and clinging blindly to it as she felt her way along to the next landing.

Finally, at the seventh floor, they reached room three of the Hawaiian Island Suite where a cardboard sign tacked to the door read: 'Absolom Mandrel Private Investigations'.

'OK,' whispered Lil. 'We've got him cornered;

we just have to get in the door long enough to tell our side of the story.'

Nedly looked doubtful.

Lil took a deep breath and knocked.

'Who is it?' a gruff voice asked.

'It's me; we met earlier, at your office.'

'It's not my office any more. Who's with you?'

Lil looked at Nedly, unsure of what to say. Nedly shrugged back at her.

'No one,' she ventured.

Abe opened the door a crack and peered out. 'Then who were you talking to just now?'

'Myself, I suppose.'

'Yeah?' The detective growled. His eye slid from side to side checking out the corridor.

'Look,' said Lil. 'I think we got off to a bad start but I do have information pertaining to one of your cases. Can I come in?'

'Nope.' Mandrel said, and pushed the door, but Lil had her foot wedged in the gap.

'Please?'

'Whatever you've got to say, you can say it from there.' He folded his arms in a way that indicated there wasn't going to be a discussion.

Lil sighed but agreed. 'OK. Have it your way.' She moved her foot away from the doorpost. 'Look, I can see you're a busy man . . .'

'That's right.' He closed the door in her face.

Lil stood there for a moment, fuming, and then flumped down against the wall opposite and folded her arms. 'We'll give him a minute.'

Nedly sat down beside her. Lil shivered. 'Maybe while we're waiting you could . . . you know.' She nodded at the door. 'You might find some info in there about your case.'

Nedly looked at it reluctantly.

'Go on. Please. We need something we can work with.'

He grimaced but stood up anyway, wriggled his shoulders and cocked his head a few times in preparation and then gingerly he put first his fingertips, and then his whole arm, through the thin wood of the door. He slid one foot in, and then the other arm and the remaining leg until just his head was left, lingering in the hallway.

105

Lil sighed. 'Just get it over with.'

Nedly gave her an annoyed look in return and then took a deep breath, closed his eyes and vanished.

A few minutes later he reappeared.

Nedly shrugged. 'There's nothing about my case; not that I could see, anyway. There are a lot of files and things but I can't open them – the only stuff I got a proper look at is a chart on the wall.

'It's a street map of Peligan City. There are pins stuck in it and newspaper clippings. He's got pictures on there too – mug shots. Some have got crosses of tape stuck over them. There are bits of string that link some of the mug shots with the newspaper articles and in the middle of it all there's a picture of this creepy-looking man.'

Lil scribbled down some notes in her book. 'Maybe it's connected to your case in some way.'

Nedly looked doubtful. 'Maybe.'

There was a slight movement behind the

fish-eye spyhole. Mandrel's voice growled out. 'That hallway is no place for a kid. Beat it, will you?' He knocked on the inside of his own door. 'Hey, I'm talking to you.'

Lil leapt up and looked back through the fish-eye at him. 'Can I come in?'

'No!'

'Then I'm not moving.'

Mandrel crashed around angrily in his apartment for a few minutes then he checked the spyhole again. She was still sitting there.

'Damn it.' He opened the door a crack. 'OK, kid, you've got ten minutes to spill it, and then you go, deal?

'Deal,' said Lil. 'It's like this; I'm on the trail of a story . . .'

Mandrel interrupted her suddenly. 'What did you say your name was?

'It's Lil.' She watched his reaction carefully for a flicker of recognition but there was nothing. 'Can I continue?' The detective nodded tetchily. '. . . about this boy who was murdered . . .'

'A murder investigation?' Mandrel nodded with mock sincerity.

'Yes . . . and now I think that your Ned Stubbs case and the investigation I'm working on are actually one and the same, so . . .' She paused, hoping to say the next bit as casually as possible – 'it makes sense that we partner up to solve it.'

'I work alone.' The detective folded his arms over his chest.

Lil tried to hide her pique with an offhand snort.

Nedly said, 'Ask him . . . about me.'

Lil shot him a look that said *I'm on it*. To Mandrel she said, 'Can I see your case file?'

'No.'

'Can you at least *tell* me what's in it?'

The detective shrugged. 'It's most likely that Stubbs ran away.'

'What if I can prove that he didn't?'

'OK,' Mandrel said slowly. Lil noticed a spark of interest appearing in his otherwise wary eyes. 'Prove it.'

Lil faltered. She tried out a line she'd heard in a film: 'I have to protect my source.'

The detective sighed and the spark went out. 'Look, if this is your idea of a tip-off I've got a shock for you, kiddo.'

Lil looked up at the grizzled old detective and pulled out what she hoped would be her big gun. 'Detective Mandrel, my hero, A. J. McNair, had this quote he used to say and they put it inside the front cover of this book about him, *McNair and the Free Press*, which happens to be my favourite book, and it says "All it takes for injustice to prevail . . ."'

'". . . is for good people to look the other way,"' Abe finished wearily. 'But no one ever said *I* was a good person.'

Lil stared him right in the eye and set her jaw, angry disappointment all over her face. 'Yeah, they did. Once they called you that. You were the long arm of the law . . . the Scourge of the Underworld. I thought you'd want to solve the case. The caretaker at the orphanage hired you to find out what happened to Ned

Stubbs. I bet you still took his money, didn't you?'

Abe Mandrel flinched. His eyes went down to the ground. 'I was hired to look into his disappearance. I looked into it. End of story.'

'When I read all that stuff about you in the paper I thought you were really somebody. But you're just like everyone else!' Lil couldn't stop herself from shouting. 'You don't care about anybody except yourself!'

Mandrel coughed. 'Sorry to disappoint you.'

'Yeah? I'll get over it!' Lil snapped and stamped off down the hall.

The detective slammed the door after her and two sunset beach prints that hung on the wall dropped to the floor. He stood on the spot for a few minutes, glaring at the fish-eye. 'Humph,' he said to himself. 'Kids today, think they know it all.'

He rehung the prints and then walked over to the window in the kitchenette and wiped an arm across the grimy pane, smearing the dirt in with the condensation. He saw the girl crossing the street below. She looked even smaller from a distance; head down, shoulders hunched, yellow coat standing out against the grey rain. She reminded Mandrel of someone. Someone he'd known long ago.

He shook his head at her. 'It's a tough lesson but better that she learns it early.'

He noticed his own reflection looking back at him in the glass; it had been a while since he last looked in a mirror. He saw the red-rimmed eyes, stubble starting to go grey, hair thinning and the dawning of a double chin. The reflection had a reproachful look in its eye.

In the kitchenette dirty plates and glasses were piled up in the sink, and the bin was overflowing with noodle cartons and polystyrene trays. Mandrel pulled off his fake hand and selected the spork attachment. He opened the carton of Singapore noodles he had picked up from the Kam Moon and started eating them. Then he stopped, unable to swallow another mouthful.

He heard a creak in the hallway outside and turned to see a slip of paper sneaking under the door. It was a menu for the Black Pug Eatery – there was a message printed along the margin in block capitals. It read:

'MY NAME IS LIL POTKIN. YOU KNEW MY MOTHER. THE NITE JAR CAFE. 7 P.M. SHARP. BRING CASE FILE.'

The note was folded round a photograph. It was the old gang before it all went sour. He saw himself as he was then, square-jawed, bright-eyed and grinning, and there beside him was Lil's mother, Naomi. The detective swallowed hard. *I knew that kid had looked familiar.* Somewhere deep inside his chest his heart lurched painfully. He gave himself a thump there and coughed.

Carefully he tucked the photograph into the frame of one of the Hawaiian sunsets and stood there looking at it until the light began to fade.

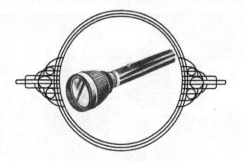

Chapter 10

The Nite Jar Cafe

The Nite Jar was an old-time diner with a long white marble counter and rows of booths upholstered in red leather. The walls were mint green, the floor was chequered in black and white tiles and the coffee was always hot and strong.

It was just after 7 p.m. and the juke box was playing ragtime jazz. Lil and Nedly had taken a window booth and ordered two ginger beers. Every few minutes Lil wiped the sleeve of her

sweatshirt across the window, leaving an arc of almost clear glass to look through at the drizzle-blurred line of traffic that crawled past as the grey early-evening light darkened towards night.

Someone had left a copy of the *Herald* behind on the table. Nedly was reading the front-page story out loud.

Security Guard Killed by Exploding Car!
In the early hours of this morning, fifty-six year old security guard Antonio McConkey was killed when his car unexpectedly exploded into a ball of flames outside City Hall.

An initial report suggests the vehicle had been leaking petrol and by turning the key in the ignition, McConkey must have caused the spark that ignited it.

Despite the close proximity to City Hall, a police spokesman has stated that they can find no evidence to suggest that the explosion was the result of terrorist action.

'Is that the fire your mum was talking about this morning?'

'Probably. Although Mum said she put that fire out with the mayor's sheepskin coat, which doesn't seem likely if it was an exploding car.' Lil took a large gulp of ginger beer.

Nedly watched her with an envious look in his eye.

She felt his gaze and stopped drinking. 'Why did you want me to order you one if you weren't going to drink it?'

'I am going to drink it.'

Lil glanced over her shoulder to check that no one was looking and then slid the bottle towards him. 'Go on, then.'

Nedly stretched out his fingers but they just delved through the bottle as he tried to take it. He sighed despondently. 'Forget it.'

'You turned the pages of the newspaper, didn't you?'

'I would probably just knock the bottle over.'

'So?'

'The ginger beer would go everywhere.'

'Big deal, I'll get a cloth. It's worth a try, isn't it? Maybe there's a knack to it.'

He gave her a tired look.

Lil pushed the bottle closer. 'Go on. Try it.'

Nedly looked like he wanted to hope and was afraid to. He wiggled his fingers and, warming up, he steepled and stretched them. He took a deep breath, cleared his throat, and tried again. He wrapped one hand round the bottle.

'That's great. Can you feel it?'

'Kind of.'

Lil leant in until she was eye-level with the bottle. She could see Nedly's fingers hovering a fraction of an inch from the glass. 'You're not actually touching it.'

'I can't do it,' he moaned.

'Not if you don't actually try.'

Nedly shook his head at her and then closed his hand. It disappeared through the glass and became a ginger-beer-coloured fist.

'OK, so that's going to take some work.' Lil pushed the bottle to one side. 'But there's loads of other stuff you can do that ordinary people

117

can't.' She glanced up and met the gaze of a couple sitting holding hands at a table on the other side of the cafe. They looked away quickly when they realised she had seen them.

Nedly raised his eyebrows at her. 'Like what?'

Lil picked up the newspaper and pretended to read the front-page story again.

'Like what?' Nedly repeated. 'Lil? Lil!'

'What?' Lil hissed, lifting the paper so she could hide behind it. 'People are staring.'

'So? Are you just going to ignore me then?'

'No,' Lil muttered through gritted teeth. 'I just forgot that no one else can see you.'

'Like, what else can I do?' Nedly persisted.

Lil propped her head up on one elbow and cupped her hand to hide her mouth. 'Like, you can give people the creeps.'

Nedly sunk his head into his hands. 'Great.'

Lil continued, 'And you're invisible.'

'Again, *great*.'

'It *is* great. You can sneak around and find stuff out, follow people without being seen. That's really useful.'

'Useful for you, maybe.' He peered at her from between his fingers.

'That's why we make such a good team,' Lil grinned. 'How about that stuff you can do with the lights? Making them flicker and go out.'

'That's not on purpose, it just happens.'

'But you know what it means? You can affect electricity. I bet you could learn how to influence radios, TVs . . .' Lil's eyes lit up. '*Tape recorders*. Hey, you could hide out up at City Hall and . . .'

Her chain of thought was broken by a shadow falling across the table. She looked up to see Abe Mandrel standing outside, staring at her through the steamed-up windows, rainwater dribbling from the brim of his battered brown trilby. Lil beckoned at him to join them.

The detective peeled off his wet coat and hung it over the seat. He pulled a paper folder out of the plastic bag he was carrying and placed it on the table. It was Nedly's file.

Nedly stared at it, full of hope and apprehension at what it might hold and then he let out a strangled yelp as the detective flumped suddenly onto his lap, completely enveloping him. Nedly scooted quickly into the corner as, with a shriek, Mandrel jumped back up like a jack-in-the-box and glared, pasty-faced, at the empty seat. Then, his cheeks reddening, Mandrel eased himself back down again, shuddered once and tried to regain his composure.

He and Lil sat there for a moment in silence, staring each other out until Mandrel went for the draw and, reaching with his left hand, pulled the photograph from the breast pocket of his suit jacket. 'Here,' he said. 'I figured you might want this back.'

'Keep it.' Lil shrugged with feigned nonchalance. 'Means nothing to me.'

Nedly snorted but she ignored him.

Mandrel stared down at the photo. 'This was taken right here at the Nite Jar, you know? That big table right over there.' He held the picture up so that Lil could compare the backgrounds. 'It was the last time we were all together,' he said grimly, placing it back on the table. 'We thought we had it all worked out back then.' He nodded at Nedly's ginger beer. 'Is that for me?'

'No!' said Nedly.

Lil nodded helplessly.

Mandrel picked it up and took a couple of swigs while Nedly flapped his hands at the bottle trying to grab hold of it so he could wrestle it away. The ginger beer began to churn, the glass trembled, and Mandrel tried to steady it and failed, splashing himself in the face. 'Damn shakes!' he swore, dabbing his chin with his tie.

'I almost had it!' Nedly was triumphant. 'Did you see?'

'Pretty good,' murmured Lil.

'All right!' the detective grumbled. 'So, I spilt a bit on my chin, no big deal. I prefer a hot cup of Java anyway.' He raised his left hand for the waitress at the bar with two fingers up. The waitress brought the coffee straight away along with a large plate of Danish pastries. Her lips and nails were post-box red, her hair curled under into a smooth blonde helmet.

'Long time no see, Abe.'

Mandrel began to wave a hello and then hesitated, looking at his hand attachment as though he was seeing it for the first time, and then he hid it under the table. The waitress gave him a quick smile and went back to the counter.

'So, anyway, you're Naomi's kid.' He ran a hand down his banana-patterned tie. 'Has she ever mentioned me?

'Never,' Lil said through a mouthful of pastry.

Mandrel looked crestfallen, then lifted his coffee and took a big swig for something to do. Nedly stared menacingly at an apricot custard. The plate of Danish started to vibrate but Mandrel didn't seem to notice.

'She never talks about the old days,' Lil explained. 'Not any of it.'

'Well, it was a long time ago, I suppose.' He gave the pecan slice on his plate a doleful look and then picked it up and took a mouthful.

The apricot custard suddenly flew from the plate, hit the window and slid down to the floor, leaving a trail of pale orange slime on the glass.

'I hate those ones,' said Lil.

'I would have eaten it.' Mandrel picked up the photograph again. 'You know this is a bit of history, right here; a week after this shot was taken everything changed.' He slid the photograph away into his pocket. Lil watched it sink from sight like a setting sun. 'We all lost something when McNair went down. Peligan lost hope.' He stirred his coffee, looking down into the dark brown liquid as though it were a portal to another time.

Lil's heart beat a little faster. 'You knew McNair?'

Mandel gave her a curious look. 'You could say that.'

'Back in the good old days?'

'Back when we thought that politicians were clean, law enforcement was fair and the press was free to report the news.' He gave a grim laugh. 'Turns out we were living in a dream. After McNair we woke up to find that the kingpins had got their dirty fingers in all the pies and there was nothing left for the rest of us to eat.' Mandrel slugged back the rest of his coffee and swallowed it like a bitter pill. 'It was just my rotten luck that the justice system was the dirtiest pie of them all.'

Suddenly the pastries didn't look that appetising. Lil pushed the plate away from her towards Nedly but he backed away, sinking further into the upholstery.

'Is that why your case against the Lucan Road Mob collapsed?'

Mandrel flashed Lil a sharp look. 'What do you know about that?'

'Just what I've read.'

'Mob boss Ramon LeTeef was known to be as slippery as an eel, but I got him – my case was watertight.' With another gulp he emptied the cup. 'Only, he must have had some powerful friends because when it got to trial the ratfink turned on the rest of the mob and vanished. After he split, his fellow mobsters starting singing. Each of them managed to

124

cop plea bargains for lesser sentences – all except one: LeTeef's partner in crime, this weird fish called Cornelius Gallows. He was what we in the force call "an evil genius". Gallows lost his head in the trial and wound up shouldering most of the charges; the judge took one look at him and sent him down to Rorschach Asylum. He died in a fire there two years later.'

Nedly shivered.

'But LeTeef never served a day.'

Lil took a long gulp of ginger beer and then asked, 'So where is he now?'

The old detective shook his head despairingly. 'No idea. He's probably in the witness protection scheme, been given a new identity, the works. They just let him go, even after he . . .' He looked miserably at his prosthetic hand. 'They called it "resisting arrest" but he shattered all the bones in my hand when I tried to stop him getting away. Shut the car door on me. *Seven times*. He knew that was the only way to get me to let go. I might have lost my hand but

125

I'm never going to let him rest, not until he's in jail, where he belongs.'

Out of the corner of her eye Lil saw Nedly turn his attention to the brown folder.

'Lil!' he hissed. 'Lil! Can you open the file for me so I can take a peek?'

Ignoring him, Lil took a bite out of her pastry and chewed on it thoughtfully. 'Is that why you quit the police force?'

Mandrel frowned. 'It felt more like they quit me. I've been working for myself for a while now and, let me tell you, I don't pay well. But I'm not giving up. LeTeef escaped justice once – he won't a second time.'

Nedly flicked at the file with a ghostly finger and the paper inside rustled invitingly.

Mandrel gave an unconscious shudder and continued speaking. Nedly was glaring at the file, the cover gaped a few times like fish gills gasping for air, but Mandrel didn't notice; he was too wrapped up in his story.

'I hadn't had a whiff of a clue to LeTeef's whereabouts until these fires started.'

Lil raised an eyebrow. 'The nurse and the security guard?'

'They're just the latest, the ones that ended in death made the papers but there have been more than thirteen mysterious fires in Peligan over the last year, and they have all targeted former members of the Lucan Road Mob. Of course most of them have different identities now, but I know that crowd, so I've been following it, joining the dots. Whoever the Firebug is, he's going to lead me straight to LeTeef.'

For the first time Lil saw something of the old Scourge of the Underworld in the grizzled detective. She reached across the table and took his hand. It was the prosthetic one but that didn't matter. 'I'll help you find him,' she said.

The detective's eyes started to fill up and he looked away and cleared his throat. He gave her a look that said he would have squeezed hers back if he had that kind of mechanism available to him.

Out of the corner of her eye Lil saw the cover

of the file swing spookily open like a trap door. She slapped her hand down on top of it, shutting the file with a bang, and making Mandrel jump.

'But first, we need to solve the Ned Stubbs case,' she said quickly, and then slapped the table again for emphasis.

Mandrel sighed and blew out his cheeks. 'I told you already. That case went cold.'

Lil gave him a stern look. 'You let it go cold. Show me the case notes.'

Reluctantly Mandrel reached inside the folder and pulled out a single sheet of paper. 'Knock yourself out.' He handed it over.

Lil read it through; it didn't take long. 'This is it?' She flattened it out on the table so Nedly could see.

Case File #112
Ned Stubbs
Status: Missing.
Address: Hawks Memorial Orphanage, Bun Hill, Peligan City West
Family: None. Guardian is Mr E. Kolchak.

Address as above.

Other information:

The rest was blank.

'This is it?' Nedly echoed Lil. 'We sat through that whole story for *this*?' He flopped face-down into the plate of pastry crumbs.

'Don't you have anything?' Lil asked. 'Any leads at all?'

'There *were* no leads. The boy just disappeared. I hate to break it to you, kid, but in Peligan City stuff like that happens all the time.'

'Not on my watch.' Lil gulped back the rest of her ginger beer and then banged the bottle back down on the table. 'Someone killed Ned Stubbs and you're just going to have to take my word for that until I can prove it to you,' she added darkly.

The detective gave her a strange look: irritation traced with nostalgia. 'You're not going to give up, are you?'

She folded her arms and looked him hard in the eye. 'Never.'

'You know, you're a lot like her – your mum, I mean.'

Lil's cheeks turned pink as she untucked her hair and flattened it. 'I know. It's the ears.'

Mandrel snorted, lips curled in a rusty smile. 'That's not what I meant, but yeah – you've got her ears too.' He rootled around in his pocket and pulled out a crumpled five-pound note and some coins and laid them on the table. He picked up the discarded *Herald* that Lil had been reading earlier, ran an eye over the cover story and then rolled it up and stuffed it in his pocket. 'Anyways, why all the interest? Who's Ned Stubbs to you?'

'He's my friend.'

'*Was* your friend.' Mandrel got to his feet, perched his hat back on the top of his head, and swung the cafe door open to the rain-splattered world beyond. 'You said he was dead, remember?'

Chapter 11

Liberating the Zodiac

Once he was out on the street Abe Mandrel's mood seemed to darken with the failing light. He turned his collar up, pulled the brim of his hat down and with no more than a mumbled 'See you', began doggedly sploshing through puddles that everyone else went out of their way to avoid.

'Come on, Nedly. He's not shaking us off that easily. Hey!' Lil shouted, running after him. 'Hey!'

Nedly ran up behind Mandrel and tried to get his attention by laying a hand on his shoulder. Mandrel spun round and staggered. He searched the empty space that surrounded him. Rain pattered on his hat, and ran down his face.

He looked at Lil. 'Did you see that?'

'What?'

'I don't know. Something.' Still looking around, he took off his hat, pulled a dirty-looking handkerchief out of his pocket in a shower of crumbs, and wiped his head with it. 'I've had a weird cloud hanging over me ever since I got to the Nite Jar.'

Nedly gave an apologetic shrug.

'You'll get used to it,' Lil murmured and winked encouragingly at Nedly.

They turned into the Paradise Street All-Night Bus Station and Mandrel joined one of the queues; there was no room left in the shelter so he stood awkwardly at the edge. A steady stream of rain fell from the guttering of the shelter and pooled on the crown of his trilby before trickling over the brim. He pulled out the copy of the *Herald* that he had taken from the Nite Jar and held it over his head like a roof. Lil stood patiently beside him, protected by the hood of her yellow mac, while Nedly hung back awkwardly at the edge of the queue like the party-goer no one wants to dance with. All around them people were shrugging their coats up and fastening the top buttons against the sudden cold as Nedly's presence began to take its toll. A woman in a hat shuddered and her baby started to cry.

'So, where are we going?' Lil asked Abe.

Mandrel gave her a heavy sigh and begrudgingly held the *Herald* open wider so it covered Lil too. 'Don't you have to be home for tea or something?'

'Mum won't be home yet; she's working late. So there won't be any tea,' she added. 'But I suppose if you don't want to kick around with me I can just go home and sit in the dark on my own until she gets back.'

Mandrel ground his teeth. 'I don't have time

to babysit.' Lil gave him a hurt look and the old detective softened slightly. 'I've got business to attend to.'

The 64A to Peligan industrial estate via the docks arrived and Abe tipped his hat back and pulled a few coins and some old fluff out of his pocket and paid his fare. Lil followed suit and nodded to Nedly to climb aboard.

'What kind of business?'

'I've got to pick up my car. I'm going to need it if we're reopening the Stubbs case; the orphanage is on the outskirts of town.'

Lil gave Nedly a triumphant thumbs-up, which was awkwardly returned by a man in overalls who thought she had aimed it at him.

As they made their way down the narrow aisle Mandrel pulled out a small hipflask from his inside pocket and took a swig. He swung into a seat near the back and looked out of the window while Nedly took the seat behind and Lil piled in next to him. She tapped Mandrel on the shoulder.

'Is your car at the garage?'

'Nope.'

'Did you lend it to someone?'

'Nope.' He bent down to wave his hand over the heater panel under the seat. 'The lousy thing isn't even on!' He kicked at it with a scuffed shoe. 'What's wrong with this bus – it's freezing in here!' As if to prove the point, tiny crystals of ice started to form on the misty window. 'Nothing works in this town!'

Lil grinned at Nedly who was leaning forward, his elbows resting on the back of Mandrel's seat. She waited a minute for the detective to stop huffing and puffing then tapped him on the shoulder again.

'I'll just tag along,' Lil assured him. 'You won't even know I'm here.'

Mandrel huddled down in his coat and rested his head on the window. He swore when the glass gave him freezer burn and Lil saw the lobes of his ears go scarlet, and then he buried his chin in the collar of his coat and pretended to be asleep.

Lil watched the city lights get further and

further away as they headed out of town towards the river.

They disembarked at the docks. Mandrel waited for the bus to pull away again and the workers who were on shifts to disperse towards their various places of work, then he ambled off to the left. He wandered for a few steps between the harbour wall and a patchy rubbish-strewn hedge and then dropped and rolled through a gap in the branches.

Lil walked after him.

'What are you doing?' she asked.

'Get down!'

Lil crouched down and shuffled over. She whispered, 'What are you doing?'

'I told you I'm just here to fetch my car.'

In front of them was a high wire-mesh security fence topped with barbed spirals. Behind the fence the concrete sloped up gradually and row after row of car windscreens glinted.

Lil squinted at the 'Beware of the Dog' signs. 'Is this some kind of car park?'

'This isn't a car park; it's a . . .' He tried to find the words. 'My car is . . .'

Lil noticed the Peligan City Police insignia on the gate. 'Impounded?'

'Nice work, Sherlock.' Mandrel stashed his prosthesis in his inside pocket and opened up a wire cutter on his Swiss Army hand. 'A misunderstanding between myself and a loan company.'

'And now we're going to steal your car back?'

'One, *we're* not going to do anything – what kind of irresponsible moron would I look like if you get caught breaking the law when I'm supposed to be looking out for you? And more importantly, two, stealing is taking someone else's property. This is my car. I'm going to liberate it.' He got down on his knees and crawled up to the fence in front of one of the 'No Entry' signs and began painstakingly snipping though the sturdy wires that formed the mesh one by one.

Snip. Snip. Snip. The wires were so tough and close together it took ten minutes for him to cut a twelve-inch slit in the security fence.

'This is going to take you all night.' Lil stood over him, watching as his jaw clenched and unclenched as though he was chewing on something bitter and hard to swallow.

'I bet I can get in there and find it,' Nedly offered.

Lil gave him an encouraging wink and then said to Abe, 'How are you even going to find it? There must be hundreds of cars in there.'

Mandrel stopped cutting, tipped his hat back and wiped the sheen of sweat off his brow. 'Do you mind giving me a bit of room? It so happens that I've got a plan.' He reached into his coat pocket and pulled out a crumpled map. He laid it on his lap and switched on a pen torch, which he held in his teeth like a cigar. The tiny spotlight traced the layout of the car park with all the grids marked.

He turned the paper and then turned it again, trying to work out which way up it went. He garbled something unintelligible. Lil took the torch from him.

'I said, the pound is divided into areas. Some

cars are here for forensic work, some have been involved in accidents, some have been . . . Well, anyway, this map will show me whereabouts they are parked. My car would have come in last night so it will be on the end of a row.' Lil looked at him sceptically. 'Don't sweat it, kiddo. I know how stuff like this works. I was a police officer, remember?' He prised open the wire on either side of the hole he had created as far as it would go.

'So you tell me,' Lil muttered to herself as she watched the big man in his rumpled mac with the sole coming away from his left shoe, try to squeeze his way through the hole in the fence, snagging the cuff of his sleeve on a metal spoke and tearing it. 'That hole is too small for you, detective,' she said helpfully.

He glared back at her, and then tried to reverse. 'Tell me something I don't know.'

'I can do better than that,' said Lil. 'I can go in for you.'

'I can cut a bigger hole,' the detective countered.

'If you've got all night. Come on, Abe . . . You don't mind if I call you Abe, do you?'

'As it happens, I do –'

'Abe,' Lil continued, 'I'll bet I can find your car in the time it would take you to cut that hole big enough to squeeze through.' She winked again at Nedly. Abe blew out his cheeks and then deflated them with a sigh. He looked irritably at the mass of cars, the too-small hole in the wire fence and then, finally, at Lil. 'Trust me, you need my help here,' she said. 'You keep working on the fence. I'll find the car.'

Before he could answer she had snatched the map and the torch from his hand and nodded Nedly through the gap, following him before Abe could work out what was happening. He barely had time for a 'What makes you think you can . . .' before she vanished.

A second later she stuck her head back through the hole. 'Just one question. What kind of car are we looking for?'

Abe hesitated. 'It's a turquoise Ford Zodiac with a busted back light, and the lock on the passenger side doesn't work. And . . . there's a bunch of plastic coconuts hanging on the rear-view mirror.'

Lil clung to the edges of the car park, holding on to the wire fence as she moved away from the gap. 'Can you find it, Nedly?'

'I'm on it.' He ran through the centre of the car park, pausing at each gap in the grid to check for the Zodiac.

Lil watched him fade into the evening light. Once his footsteps died away he was only a glimmer in the shadows; a minute later and there was no sign of him at all. The car park was silent but for the sounds of the nearby docks: rigging clanking in the breeze and the odd gull screeching as it flew overhead. The water gave off the salt and ammonia smell of the sewers. A whistle cut through the night air. Lil looked in the direction of the sound and saw a shadow coalesce into a boy shape waving his arms over his head.

'It's here!' cried Nedly as she drew near.

The Zodiac had seen better days. The side

panels were dented and scored, rust was creeping up from under the wheel arches, the rear bumper was missing, the front tyre looked flat and the number plate was only held on by one screw.

'I can't believe this is actually the one he wants back,' said Lil. 'There must be another turquoise Zodiac here. We'll have to keep looking.'

Nedly was peering in through the windscreen. 'It's the one.' He pointed at the three plastic coconuts that dangled from the rear-view mirror like a clutch of shrunken heads.

'Classy,' grinned Lil.

'Shhh,' hissed Nedly, glancing over his shoulder. 'Someone's there!' They saw the flicker of a torch – a white beam dancing along the furthest fence. It blinked as the bearer turned it towards them. Nedly pointed to the car. Lil nodded. She crept round to the passenger's side, where the lock was busted, pulled at the handle and crawled inside, closing the door quietly behind her. The foot well was a nest of discarded stake-out materials: empty cardboard cups, greasy brown-paper bags and serviettes with old ketchup stuck to them. Lil crawled over it all to the relatively clean driver's side and crouched down beside the pedals.

A dog started barking. Lil peered out through the window. A few rows away she could see a sleek black-and-tan Rottweiler with a spiked leather collar pulling a guard towards them on a heavy chain. The guard's torch beam bounced along the windscreens and windows of the parked cars as they passed each one.

The dog stopped suddenly, twitched its long black nose and let out a rumbling growl like an engine ticking over. It whipped its head round towards the Zodiac and then it launched itself in Lil's direction, almost dragging the guard off his feet. When it was close enough that Lil could see the foam dripping from its jaws she heard Nedly nervously clear his throat and then step out of the shadows towards it. As he approached, the hound skidded to a halt, pinned its ears back, and the fur on its haunches rose. With a throaty snarl its black lips peeled back to reveal pink gums and sharp white fangs.

Lil gasped and ducked down as low as she could get. She fumbled to lock the door, her hand trembling, and jammed her head under the steering wheel.

The growl grew louder and more menacing. Lil could hear the guard saying, 'What is it, girl?' as the dog snapped at the air in front of it.

She heard Nedly's frightened voice yelling: 'I'm going to draw them off. Get ready to run, Lil.' Then she heard his footsteps pounding away. There was a shout followed by the zip and clatter of a metal chain being pulled out of someone's hand and then dragged across concrete by a dog running at full pelt. The sound travelled further away, pursued by the beat of the guard's footsteps as he tore after it.

Lil breathed out with relief. She pulled at the door handle and leant forward to climb out but her hood snagged on something under the steering wheel and yanked her backwards. She grabbed it and pulled herself free. She opened the door and saw the slick concrete of the car park roll by beneath her as the car lurched slowly forward. She had to stare at it for a moment before she realised what was happening. She gulped, slammed the door and climbed up onto the seat.

Although she was riding low and the docks area was poorly lit, Lil could still see the silver glint of a row of parked cars ahead. The Zodiac was moving slowly down through the car park, veering towards them.

Lil had never driven an actual car before but she'd been on the dodgems at the amusement park a couple of times so she understood steering, and that was all she could do. She heaved the wheel to the right and almost missed the last car in the row, clipping its rear bumper; the impact sent her veering towards the grid of cars on the other side. The Zodiac careened onwards, picking up speed.

Lil slid down, stretched her legs into the foot well and struck out for a pedal but the seat was too far back and she couldn't make herself let go of the steering wheel. She wrestled it from side to side, trying to get it to straighten up but she couldn't get the right balance and the Zodiac began slaloming. Out of the corner of her eye she caught sight of Abe clambering through the hole in the fence. He stared at her in disbelief as she drifted past the last row of cars and then she saw him mouth a swear word before turning on his heel and trying to squeeze his way back through the gap, clutching his hat.

Lil looked back ahead just in time to see the metal gates approaching and braced herself for impact. The Zodiac busted through with a rusty clang and a shower of sparks. When she peered out from the cradle of her arms she saw Nedly standing right in her path, waving his arms madly – the universal signal for STOP!!!! She hauled the steering wheel round, turning a hard left to avoid him, and narrowly missed the harbour wall. The sudden change in direction acted like a brake, and the car slowed down.

Abe stumbled alongside for a few paces, trying to get the driver's-side door open as the car ambled to a halt. He hurled himself inside, narrowly missing Lil, who had to dive for the passenger seat. She could see the Tinker Bell light of the guard's torch dancing through the car park towards them and heard a shrill whistle on the wind and the savage barking of the dog that answered it.

Huffing and puffing, Abe folded down the wire cutters and pulled out his driving-attachment pincers.

'Come on!' Lil urged. The guard was gaining on them; flashes of white torchlight strobed in through the rear window.

Abe flipped down the sun shade and the key dropped into his waiting pincer; he stuck it in the ignition and gave it a sharp turn. The car spluttered into life, the radio began blasting out calypso music at high volume and one of the windscreen wipers swung furiously into action.

They snaked up the track in a cloud of dust,

burning fuel and tyres. Lil was whooping. Abe managed a relieved grimace.

He hit the lights and the harbour came into view alongside them, picked out by the two dim yellow beams. As they sped up the gravelly dock road Lil looked back through the rear window at the pinprick of blinking torchlight, which disappeared as they rounded a bend – and then all she could see was the stony path receding in the red glow of the single working back light.

A draught of chill air enveloped the car. Ice crystals formed at the damp edges of the windscreen. The radio station re-tuned to static and then back to the calypso band, and with a pop Nedly materialised in Lil's lap.

She shrieked, 'Yah!'

Abe slammed on the brakes. He turned to her with an ashen face. 'What?

Nedly scrambled off Lil and over to the back seat.

'Nothing,' said Lil, trying to get her breath back. She had broken out in a cold sweat and her heart was racing. 'It was just delayed shock.'

The detective observed her. 'Are you OK? You don't look so good.'

'I'm fine really.' She peered over her shoulder at Nedly and gave him a look that said: *Don't ever do that again.*

Nedly shrugged meekly. 'I'm sorry I scared you.'

'It's OK,' Lil murmured. 'It was pretty cool actually.'

Abe slanted a look across. 'I was hoping for a more subtle exit, but you got the job done.' Then he added gruffly, 'Good work, I suppose.'

Lil grinned. 'Really?'

'I just said so, didn't I?' Abe hit the heating vent a couple of times. 'Lousy thing is broken.' He shrugged his mac closer around him and turned up the collar.

Lil put up the hood on her sweatshirt and settled back in her seat as they wound their way towards the bright lights of the city. She stole a grin at Nedly and then closed her eyes and let the growl of the engine rock her to sleep.

Chapter 12

The Hawaiian Island Incident Room

The next day was Sunday. Nevertheless Lil got up bright and early, ready to begin work on the Ned Stubbs case. She collected Nedly from his sleeping quarters in the airing cupboard on the first-floor landing and they went down to breakfast only to find that her mother had already left.

There was a note pinned to the fridge door:

Sorry, had to go into work again (the last weekend, I promise!).

Big project, almost finished.

Mum x

Lil crumpled it up and stuffed it in her pocket. 'If she was here I'd probably have to tell her about me running into Abe. But she's not here so . . .' She shrugged. 'I suppose it can wait.'

Peligan City was bleary with rain as they took the 9.25 bus downtown. On the corner of Shoe Street and Spindle Lane, a newspaper seller was changing the front-page story on his board. Lil paused under the awning of his stall to read the bold black writing: 'Doctor Killed in Prison Office Inferno!'

'Another fire,' Nedly pointed out.

'That's the third one this week. I wonder if it's another of the old mobsters.'

On the seventh floor of the Mingo, Abe answered the door on Lil's twelfth knock. He fired his best glower at her through eyes that were drooping and bloodshot. His hair was sticking up like a hen's backside and yesterday's stubble had sprouted into a tufty beard overnight. 'What time do you call this?' he growled.

'This is what we call *morning*,' said Lil chirpily, darting under his arm and into the room beyond.

'Make yourself at home, why don't you?' he called after her.

Hawaiian Island Suite Three couldn't have looked less homely. On every available surface were clusters of empty bottles and dirty glasses, plates and piles of old newspapers. The palm-leaf-patterned carpet was strewn with pizza boxes and there were mounds of crumpled laundry balled up in torn plastic bags on the settee.

'You actually live here?'

The detective looked affronted. 'Well, I work here and sleep here, if that's what you mean. It's plenty good enough for me. Times are tough, kiddo.'

Lil spotted the twin set Hawaiian sunset prints on the wall behind him.

'They're nice,' she said lamely, pointing at them.

The detective didn't look round. 'They came with the place, obviously.'

Lil wiped a strip of grime off one of the windows that looked down onto the street. Clouds of steam billowed up from the noodle bar downstairs, and over the line of shirts that were hanging outside.

'It gets the creases out of them,' Abe said, and then frowned at himself.

'Can we have the fire on, Abe? I'm soaked,' said Lil.

'Don't worry about it; you're not staying long.'

Lil shivered. Abe sighed and shook his head but he knelt by the gas fire and lit it with a match. 'I'm not made of money, you know. I suppose you want a drink too?'

Lil glanced at the almost empty bottles. 'Um, water please – or tea. Tea would be nice.'

Abe pulled open the curtain that divided the kitchenette from the rest of the bedsit and started rattling about with some crockery. As soon as he'd disappeared, Lil nodded Nedly towards Abe's desk and filing cabinet. Nedly stood his ground, looking like he hadn't understood.

'Don't pretend you don't understand me,' Lil hissed. 'Have a poke around while he's out of the way.'

Abe stuck his head through the curtain. 'Did you just say something to me?'

Lil flashed him an honest smile. 'I just wondered if there were any biscuits.'

'There aren't.' He closed the curtains again.

Nedly whispered, 'No way, Lil. We're guests – it's not polite to go poking around in other people's stuff.'

'I'm the guest. He doesn't even know you're here.' Nedly looked hurt. 'Just see if there is anything about your case, that's all. Check on a few of the cupboards and desk drawers; see if he's hiding anything.'

'It doesn't look like he's hiding anything,' Nedly said doubtfully. 'It looks as if most of his belongings are here on the floor.

'Are you going to tell him about the latest fire, the one at the prison?'

Lil pursed her lips and gave a quick shake of the head. 'We don't want him to get side-tracked now that he's finally back on your case. We'll tell him later.'

'He'll see it on the newsstand anyway.'

'We'll distract him,' Lil said confidently. 'Come on.' She pointed to a tall metal cabinet propped up against the wall. 'You look in there; I'll check out these files.'

One corner of the room obviously functioned as the 'office' since he had downsized from 154c Wilderness Lane. Collapsed towers of files and cardboard document boxes were stacked high alongside leaning rows of lever-arch folders spilling pages of notes and photographs, and boxes of tapes without cases.

Lil was drawn to a dusty typewriter on the desk. 'Nice typewriter,' she called out, wincing as she kicked over a number of glass bottles lined up by the chair. 'I mean it. It's an Olympia

SM-3. I'm going to get one of those. One day,' she added quietly.

The bitterness in Abe's disembodied voice carried through the closed curtain. 'It was a retirement present. I can't even type.'

On the wall behind the desk Lil examined the map that Nedly had described on his previous visit. He had been right: this was nothing to do with his case, it was Abe's record of the activities of the Peligan City Firebug. News clippings about arson attacks and other miscellaneous fires were pinned to it like moths, and a half-made cobweb of brown woollen threads connected the scenes with old mug shots of the Lucan Road Mob. In the centre was a photograph of Abe's nemesis, Ramon LeTeef. His skin was pale and chalky-looking and his hair was white like lamb's wool. His teeth, which looked grey in the black-and-white picture, were filed to sharp points and he was baring them in a snarl for the camera. He reminded Lil of a picture she had once seen of an anglerfish: all teeth and small eyes staring out from the murk.

On the floor below the map, on top of a partially unravelled brown pullover, was a bloated box file labelled 'Lucan Road Mob'. Lil picked it up and started thumbing her way through. She gazed at the mug shots of the nurse Shirley Kreutz, aka Cold Shirl, and the security guard, Antonio McConkey, aka Lay z Boy. Both had black crosses obscuring their faces, marking them out as deceased.

She found pictures and descriptions of the other mobsters holding up crime identification numbers. Cornelius Gallows had a single wisp of hair sticking up on top of his head, like a feather stuck on an eggshell. His eyes were large and almost colourless; they sank back beneath his hairless brow. Lil shuddered and slammed the file shut.

Nedly's head appeared through the door of a large metal cabinet. 'Nothing in here; just old photo albums and folders.'

Lil put down the file and pulled open the door of the cabinet. She reached in and picked up an album just as Abe started coming through the curtain. She threw it back and quickly shut the door on Nedly, who was trying to get out again. He transported into the room with a shudder and staggered queasily away.

Abe looked suspiciously at Lil. 'I found you a biscuit.'

'Thanks,' said Lil. Taking the tea, she took a bite and swallowed with difficulty. 'I think of prawn crackers being more like crisps than biscuits.'

'What's the difference?' Abe picked up his prawn cracker with his pliers and tried to dunk it into the tea. He gripped it too hard and the cracker snapped in half, both bits falling into the cup. He scooped it out with his good hand and winced at the scalding water.

Lil picked a book off the desk. '"Disembodiment and Existential Phenom–en–ology" by Dr C. Gallows PhD – sounds like a real pot-boiler. Have you read it?' she asked him.

'I'm not much of a reader. I've dipped in a couple of times – but it's not what you would call a page-turner.'

Lil pondered the haughty-looking photograph of Gallows wearing a bleach-white lab coat on the back cover. 'What I don't get is, why would he have associated with the Lucan Road Mob in the first place? He doesn't seem the type.'

'My guess is they were funding his research in exchange for the high-tech burglarising equipment he designed to help them in their exploits. According to his psychiatrist's testimony at the trial, Gallows was experimenting with near-death out-of-body experiences; only his hypothesis involved not just near but *actual* death experiences.'

Lil thumbed through the pages. 'What kind of experiments?'

'Well, I'm no egghead, but it was some kind of Frankenstein's-monster stuff to do with harnessing the spirit of the recently deceased.' Abe took a slug of tea and coughed on the sludge of prawn cracker that was lurking in the dregs. 'Luckily he was stopped at the animal-testing stage, before he had a chance to try it out on a human subject – otherwise they could have added first-degree murder to his list of crimes.'

Lil pondered this. 'How do they know he never tried it out on a human subject? She looked at Nedly. He shuddered and the lights in the Hawaiian Island Suite buzzed dimly.

In the kitchenette the kettle switched itself back on and started boiling furiously. Abe lumbered to his feet, hit it and it went off again. 'Because his lab was full of dead rabbits, not dead people. Anyway, he's toast now. Forget about him. We've got other fish to fry.'

'But he died in a fire too, didn't he?' Lil persisted. 'Is that just a coincidence or was he the first victim?'

Abe shrugged. 'Not my concern, or yours. I'm only looking into the Firebug because he's going to lead me to LeTeef. End of.'

Lil stared at him, disbelieving. 'But even if all his victims are mobsters it's still murder. If someone is taking them down one by one – it's still wrong. Shouldn't you be trying to stop them?'

'That's a job for the police.'

Lil snorted. 'You were police once.'

Abe gave her a grim look. 'Yeah, once, and look where it got me. Now, if you've finished lecturing me on law and order, we can get to work.'

He ploughed a heap of papers off the settee and Lil sat down. Nedly sat on the floor at a distance, his back to the palm-tree-print wallpaper, and Abe paced back and forth across a small patch of worn carpet that was free of litter. 'OK, so I know from the caretaker, Mr Kolchak, that there were no disturbances at the orphanage the night Stubbs disappeared, aside from the usual kids' stuff: lost toys, tears before bedtime, nothing serious. So we can assume that he left there by his own accord. That gives us two lines of enquiry – why did he leave, and where did he go? The first might give us an answer to the second so we'll start there.

'You say you knew the boy; can you think of any reason why he might have snuck out after dark?'

Lil looked at Nedly; he seemed thoughtful for a moment. 'I remember . . . no, it's gone. He shrugged back at her and she passed it on to Abe, who rolled his eyes.

'Nothing? How well did you know him exactly?'

'Maybe not as well as you'd think,' Lil admitted.

'So we start from square one. We need to get some background on the kid. The orphanage was a dead end. Kolchak didn't have any information about Stubbs before he arrived but there will be a record somewhere. If we could get a look at his file, find out who his parents were, where they lived, etcetera, we can start to build up a picture of who he was, and then perhaps we will be able to make an educated guess as to where he would go.'

'OK,' said Lil, unconvinced. She caught Nedly's eye but he nodded back at her in agreement. 'Let's do it.'

Abe chewed it over. 'Our problem is those files are confidential. The police or a magistrate could access them but we may have to grease some palms, and I'm all out of grease.' He caught Lil glancing at his stained tie and scowled. 'You know what I mean. Hard cash.'

'We might not need it,' said Lil. 'Mum works up at City Hall in the Public Records Department. I bet she can help.'

Nedly raised his eyebrows hopefully but Abe snorted. 'That doesn't sound like the Naomi I know.'

Lil sank back down on the settee, and a spring boinged ominously from under the cushion. 'Maybe you're right; she probably won't want to get in any trouble.' She saw Nedly wilt despondently against the wallpaper like an overcooked egg noodle. 'But everything is worth a try – right?'

She jumped to her feet and made for the door but Abe stayed put. He was stroking his almost-beard and looking thoughtful. 'Do you think she'd want to see me?'

Lil puffed out her cheeks impatiently. 'Mum? Who knows? Maybe.'

Abe looked dismally at his crumpled suit and stained tie. 'Entertain yourself for a few minutes, kid. There are a couple of things I need to do before we leave.' With that he disappeared into what Lil took to be the bathroom. Moments later they heard the sound of water running.

Lil collapsed back onto the settee and twisted her head round to look at Nedly. 'Do you really not remember anything about your life before you . . . before that night?'

He looked at her uncertainly. 'I just have this one memory – I mean, I don't know if it's a real memory. I don't like thinking about it.'

'Go on,' urged Lil.

Nedly's eyes clouded; his voice was gravelly, barely above a whisper. 'It starts with a trip, the sort of feeling that you get in a dream when you wake up before you hit the floor. Except when I wake up I'm not really awake. I'm in a corridor with hundreds of doors that all look the same and I walk slowly past them all until I reach this one – the one I have to go through.

164

I'm trying not to be scared but this creepy feeling is clinging to me like sweat. The door handle is metal; it's humming in my palm as I hold it, like its alive . . .' He paused for breath and Lil thought she could hear his heart beating frantically over the sound of Abe's electric razor. 'And that's when I realise . . . that I'm not alone. There's something in there with me, something I was looking for. It has stringy black hair, thin arms and no neck, and it's staring right at me with these white, empty eyes. And I can hear someone laughing. Then a pale blue light blinds me and there's only silence and this smell . . .'

Lil gulped noisily. 'What kind of smell?'

'Burning,' said Nedly. 'I can smell burning.'

Abe wandered in wearing a clean vest and pulled a freshly steamed shirt off the washing line outside. Lil turned to face him, her mouth still hanging open from Nedly's revelation, her eyes wide and haunted.

Frowning at her, Abe knotted a navy-blue tie patterned with flying saucers round his neck and then slapped his cheeks with a potent cologne that smelt like anti-freeze.

'Looking good,' Lil said weakly.

'All right, I scrub up the same as anyone – no need to go on about it,' he said, looking at his reflection in a spoon, before straightening his tie and adjusting his hat. 'So, we're ready to go?'

Lil glanced at Nedly, who shivered. The lights flickered on and off. Abe looked grimly up at the bulb.

'It's only a matter of time before they cut me off,' he said.

Chapter 13

City Hall

It was Sunday; City Hall was dead.

Abe, Lil and Nedly had left the Zodiac parked in the same alleyway where McConkey had exploded two nights earlier, and set off towards the glass-fronted skyscraper, which reflected the concrete buildings opposite and the mottled grey sky.

As they neared the doors Lil said, 'So, Abe, strictly speaking, I'm not actually allowed past the lobby, let alone up to the offices, so if you could, you know, distract the guard or whatever? There's a door-release button on the underside of the desk. You'll have to lean over to press it.'

Abe tried out a casual shrug. 'I thought we were both going to talk to Naomi?' Lil could see he was trying, but failing, not to sound disappointed.

'And we will,' she assured him. 'It's just better if I put her in the picture first.'

The security guard was sitting at the front desk idly turning the pages of the *Herald*, while over his head a row of CCTV monitors flicked between greyscale images of the empty corridors of City Hall.

Lil zipped up her yellow mac and pulled the hood low over her head and ducked behind a pillar.

'We need to go through that door,' she whispered to Nedly, nodding towards the stairwell. As soon as Abe hits the button we've got a four-second window. Well, I have. I guess you could just melt through the wall or something.'

'I'll take the door option,' said Nedly.

A figure appeared on one of the screens, prowling

one of the hallways, dressed in a shiny tracksuit with his auburn hair gelled back into a slick ponytail. They saw him pause for a moment to do a series of squat jumps. Craig Weasel's mania for self-improvement had resulted in a body that was two sizes too big for his narrow head. His face was pointed, with small features that gathered around a shark-fin nose. Then the screen flicked to another image and Weasel vanished.

'The mayor's bodyguard,' Lil explained. 'That means the mayor is here too. Keep your eyes peeled, Nedly. We can't afford to run into either one of them.'

Abe reached the desk and pressed the 'Ring for Attention' bell. The guard looked up, took in Abe's cheap suit, gave him a withering glance and drawled: 'Can I help you?'

'Hey, pal,' said Abe as he scanned the CCTV screens. 'I was wondering: what's it like working as a guard in one of these joints?'

'Why, are you looking for a job?'

'Me? No, I'm just curious.'

'Curious, eh? Well, it's OK – it suits me.'

Abe cast a glance back over his shoulder to check Lil was in position. 'I'll bet. Don't suppose you've got a car parked out there?' He nodded vaguely towards the entrance.

'So what if I do?'

'No reason. Just saw some young fellows out there looking suspicious. Looked like they were casing one of the cars, thought maybe they were up to something.'

'Was it the green Morris Six?'

'Yeah,' Abe ventured. 'That's the one.'

'Why those little . . . !' The guard scrambled to his feet, unlocked the hatch on the desk and charged out through the lobby. Abe tipped Lil the wink, leant over the counter and felt around until he found the button.

At the signal Lil and Nedly tore across the floor, hit the door just as the green light came on, swung it open and slipped through to the stairwell.

They were just in time as the guard staggered back into the lobby, out of breath. 'There was no one there!'

'Must have scared them off,' Abe said.

The guard eyed him suspiciously. He returned to his desk and started pressing buttons to check the CCTV screens.

'Can't be too careful these days,' Abe said. 'Nasty business, what happened to that other guy, McConkey.'

He pointed at the wall where a portrait of the deceased guard hung, his nose squashed flat as though he was pushed up against the glass of the photo frame. Overhead was a banner that read: 'We'll miss you ____' There was a gap at the end where someone had written 'Antonio' in marker pen. It looked like the kind of celebratory banner you put up when someone was retiring. Well, McConkey *had* retired. Permanently.

'Blown up in his own car.' Abe raised both eyebrows. 'Yikes! What do you make of that?'

'What's to make of it? It was a freak accident. Some kind of fuel leak, they said.'

'Must have been some leak.'

'Well, that's what I heard,' the guard replied grumpily. 'What's with all the questions?'

'Like I said, I'm just curious.'

'Well, I'm busy so maybe you could go and be curious somewhere else.'

Abe tried to think of some other way to prolong the conversation but he had run out of material and the security guard knew it. 'All right then,' he conceded. 'I'll be off. Nice talking to you.'

He was just turning to leave when the lift pinged open, revealing Mayor Dean and his bodyguard, Craig Weasel. The mayor was a small man in every sense of the word, drowning in his sheepskin jacket and the furry Russian hat that engulfed his head. A sharp pencil moustache drew a line over his unnaturally white teeth, which sparkled with a glint of gold. He had won by a landslide at his first election with his brilliant smile and glossy black hair, but that was years ago. Before he was mayor he'd been a game-show host, and before that a reality TV star and before that . . . No one knew him back then.

Weasel took in Abe with disdain. The mayor, on the other hand, froze. He stopped mid-step and then yanked Weasel back into the lift mumbling, 'Wait, I've forgotten my . . .' and started hammering on the button. Before Abe could catch the rest the doors had closed again and the lift was travelling back upstairs.

By the time they reached the twenty-first floor Lil was done in. She staggered up the last three flights and then slid to the floor on the landing, recovering her breath, legs aching, while Nedly, completely unaffected by the uphill climb, hopped restlessly from foot to foot, waiting for her to get going again. She pushed back her hood a little and peered up at him. 'Check the coast is clear, will you?'

Nedly stuck his head through the door, jumped a little and then drew it back. 'It's pretty crowded out there but I don't think there are any actual people around.'

Lil gave him a puzzled look, stepped out onto the landing and came eyeball to eyeball with a series of larger-than-life-size cardboard cut-outs of the most powerful man in Peligan City – Mayor Dean – lining the corridor like a row of paper dollies.

'Now, that's creepy,' she said with a wink. 'Come on.'

They crept past a series of framed photographs documenting Mayor Dean's political highlights, all from the early days: standing arm in arm with his predecessor, Mayor Al Davious, before Davious resigned in favour of his protégé; shaking hands with other dignitaries; opening supermarkets and casinos. Lately nothing new had opened. A lot of places had closed but that had all been done very quietly.

Ping – the lift doors opened.

Lil ducked back behind the nearest cut-out in the nick of time. Nedly froze in the middle of the corridor, fear bolting him to the floor.

Craig Weasel and Mayor Dean strode out. Weasel was trying to look steely calm but, as they passed, Lil could see he was gritting his teeth; the mayor was giving him an earful.

'Everywhere I turn there's people snooping around. I'm not even safe in my own building. What do I pay you for? And keep a closer eye on the minions; I can't move an inch in this place without that pesky news pamphlet finding out about it. We've got a mole, Weasel, and it's your job to flush them out!'

Nedly winced and then closed his eyes as the mayor and Weasel walked towards him. Weasel was the first to pass through. He spun round thinking that someone was there, and collided with the mayor, who was close behind and still ranting.

'What are you playing at, Weasel?' he spluttered.

'Nothing . . . I thought.' Weasel stepped forward again and shivered. 'There's some kind of cold spot. Right here.' He waved his hand in and out through Nedly's chest and the lights in the hallway flickered.

'What was that? Weasel, protect me!' The mayor looked stricken. 'It's him again! I might have known he wouldn't give up . . .' His eyes were darting around, searching for something. 'Not after he found a way back . . .' Lil could see beads of grey-coloured sweat dripping from his hair-line. 'Can't you feel him?' His hands were shaking when he walked up to Nedly. He stared at the space like he was looking into the abyss. Nedly looked right back at him and then blew on his face. 'Arrghh!' the mayor screamed.

Weasel frowned at him; his own pulse had started racing too. 'Keep it together, sir,' he said, talking to himself as much as the mayor. It's probably just a strange draught coming from somewhere.'

'He's here – I can feel it.' The mayor wailed. 'Get the extinguisher!'

As Weasel strode towards the fire exit he paused as he reached the cut-out that Lil was hiding behind, stuck out a finger and poked it. The model tipped backwards but didn't fall. Weasel frowned. He was just leaning over to take a look behind it when all the doors along the hall opened and slammed shut, one after the other, like a Mexican wave.

'Save me, Weasel!' whimpered the mayor, collapsing in a faint.

Weasel darted over and scooped up Mayor Dean in his arms and laid him carefully on the floor in the hallway. From behind the cut-out Lil watched him disappear into the twenty-fourth-floor bathroom for a moment and then return with a tumbler of water, cradling the mayor's head as he poured it down his throat.

'Get off me!' snapped the mayor as he came round, pushing the glass aside. 'Just get me out of here!'

Weasel bundled the shivering mayor down the hallway and into the stairwell. 'I'll take you to the refectory, sir. You'll be safe there.'

He staggered down the corridor past Lil and Nedly, who were now both hiding behind the cut-out.

As soon as the lift began its descent they breathed out a massive sigh of relief.

'Phewee! That was close,' said Lil. 'Nice work with the doors, by the way. You've been practising.'

Nedly shrugged modestly. 'It was nothing. Just throwing my energy around a bit – I didn't really know what would happen.'

'Well, you certainly freaked the mayor out.'

Nedly pondered this. 'Did you think that he looked kind of familiar?'

Lil shrugged a shoulder at him. 'The mayor? He looks like the mayor always looks. His picture is on the front cover of the *Herald* almost every day. There can't be a person in Peligan who wouldn't recognise him, although I suppose he's a bit older and wrinklier in real life.'

Nedly was watching the lift doors with a strange expression on his face. 'No, it's not that, he's –' He froze mid-sentence. 'What was that?'

There was a noise coming from the mayor's office: a clunking, scraping sound like multiple locks being turned. Someone was in there.

'Go and see,' Lil whispered to Nedly.

'No way. You go.'

Lil gave him a look. 'They'll see me.' It was

too late; a shadow flitted across the rippled glass door and it opened noiselessly. Lil scarpered through Nedly – who had been standing right behind her – with a stomach-churning shudder, and dived back behind the cut-out. A second later she heard soft footsteps crossing the plush carpet and a figure flitted past them, down the hallway to the Public Records Department.

'Mum?'

Naomi Potkin looked up sharply; her face was pale. 'Lil! You shouldn't be up here.'

Her hair was damp at the edges and her glasses had slipped down her nose. She unlocked the door to Public Records and bundled Lil inside, closing it after her. Nedly was forced to leak through the gap by the hinges.

Lil gave him a companionable grimace and then turned to her mother. 'Mum, I just need . . .'

But Naomi wasn't listening. She was bent over the photocopier. The green scanning light slid back and forth across her face, reflecting off her lenses and picking up the furrows in her brow. Lil waited patiently while her mother pulled the master documents out of the copier and shuffled them into a ledger, retrieved the copies and shoved them into an envelope. 'How did you even get in here?'

'I just need a favour,' Lil tried again. 'Some information from the Archives.'

Naomi paused. 'What are you talking about? Lil, you can't be here . . . If they find you . . .'

Footsteps thundered down the corridor and Lil barely had time to take cover behind the filing cabinet before the door burst open and Craig Weasel appeared on the threshold.

Lil's mum didn't jump. She didn't even look up. She slid the envelope she was holding into a towering pile of papers that balanced precariously on her desk and pulled at the hem of her jacket to straighten it. 'Morning, Mr Weasel.'

Craig Weasel's eye twitched. A thin smile opened up beneath his nose.

'Potkin, working overtime as always,' he said

in a slimy voice that seemed to come from his nose.

'Always plenty to do.' Naomi opened the filing-cabinet drawer, blocking Lil from view, and began rifling through paper folders.

Weasel took a step towards her; he was so close that Lil could see the veins pulsing in his temple. Naomi turned to face him.

'Are you all right, Mr Weasel?' she asked timidly. 'You seem agitated.'

Weasel's small eyes narrowed to the size of almonds. 'I was just on my way down to the refectory when I heard that there's been an intruder on the premises. Someone has activated the emergency door release.'

'Really?' Naomi didn't flinch. 'Oh dear. Where?'

Craig Weasel wrung a humourless smile out of his lips. 'Never mind. I'll find them.' His eyes slid over to the tower of papers on the desk. 'You worry about your own job.'

'Yes, Mr Weasel.' She dipped her head deferentially. 'Thank you, I will.'

As soon as he was out of earshot Lil muttered, 'What a knucklehead! Mum, I need your help – there's a file I need to see . . .' Her voice trailed off. 'What are you doing?'

Her mother was shepherding her towards the door. 'Was that you, Lil? Pushing the emergency button?'

'No, it really wasn't,' Lil replied honestly, as she tried to double back into the room.

Naomi didn't look convinced. 'I need to get you out of here. There's a fire exit at the end of the corridor. Come with me.'

'But, Mum – !'

Lil found herself being escorted back down the hallway so fast that the cut-outs wobbled as they rushed past. Nedly followed in their wake. They reached the door at the end and Naomi took Lil by the shoulders and turned her so they were face to face. 'Listen to me. You shouldn't be here. I've told you that City Hall is off-limits.'

'But, Mum – !'

Naomi rummaged in her pocket and handed

Lil some change. 'Get the bus straight home, OK? And, Lil, never, ever, do what I am about to.' With that she elbowed the fire-alarm panel and an ear-splitting siren started up. The emergency lock on the fire exit sprang open and Naomi bundled Lil out.

Chapter 14

The Best Dogs this Side of the River

They emerged from the alleyway at the back of City Hall to see Abe waiting under a street lamp on the other side of the road. The brim of his hat was down low against the drizzle, and his face was in shadow. He seemed to Lil as though he was thinking deeply or maybe even asleep.

He looked up as they approached. 'So?'

'No dice – she was busy.'

'Oh.' He kicked at a bit of gum wrapper that was stuck to his shoe.

Lil could see that he was trying to hide his disappointment so changed the subject. 'We did run into the mayor and his bodyguard in the corridor,' she told him, wincing inwardly at the 'we' that had slipped out.

'Did you get caught?' Abe hadn't seemed to notice her mistake. 'I heard alarm bells ringing.'

'No, but it was close.'

'That mayor is a strange character,' Abe mused. 'There's something about him I don't like.' He shook his head thoughtfully, as though he was trying to dislodge a memory from the cobwebbed recesses of his mind.

Lil cleared her throat to knock the detective out of his reverie and said: 'So, what now?'

'Well, the more official channels are no good without Naomi's help.' He sighed. 'All right, we'll try the orphanage again, maybe ask some of the kids if they remember anything from the night Stubbs went missing, see if he had any friends there – but first I need to get the word on the streets about something. There's been another fire, last night.'

'Really?' Lil attempted a look of total surprise.

'You heard about it then?' Abe growled. 'Thanks for telling me.'

'I forgot.' Lil shrugged, her ears reddening.

'Hmmm. Worried I'd get distracted, eh? Look, I don't even know if this one is connected. This vic wasn't on my list; he's a doctor, a real one, so why would the Firebug target him? Something doesn't add up.' He scratched his chin. 'I need more information. Come on, let's eat.'

'Ice cream?' Lil said hopefully. 'You could treat me. What do you say?'

Abe scowled at the sky and turned up his collar. 'I say it's raining. How about we settle for a hot dog?'

The hot dog stand was on the corner of Fig Street where a steady stream of traffic crawled by in a chorus of blaring horns. The city stretched up from the pavement, its lights reflected by puddles, a fairground of colours from the traffic signals and advertising bill-boards to the office tower blocks that loomed like giant dominoes.

Mist blew around the hot dog cart, mixing with the steam from the grill. The vendor wore a pillbox hat and an apron over a shiny blue tracksuit. Her face was peppered with freckles and she had three watches strapped to her right arm.

Abe sidled up to her with a nod. 'Hey, Minnie.'

She looked up with a double take and then smiled a genuine yellow-toothed grin. 'Well, look who it is! Detective Absolom Mandrel as I live and breathe.'

Abe adjusted his hat. 'How's tricks?'

'Same old, same old.' A semi-awkward silence descended. 'It's been a while.'

'Yeah, I've been busy.'

'I heard that.' Minnie flipped over a shovel full of onions on the hotplate.

Abe gave a grim snort. 'You always did have big ears, Minnie.'

Minnie winked and then pointed a thumb at Lil. 'So, who's this?'

'Mind your beeswax.'

Lil stepped closer and breathed in the warm onion and sausage smell. 'I'm Lil, Mandrel's associate.' She murmured out of the corner of her mouth to the detective: 'You don't mind if I call you Mandrel, do you?'

Abe muttered back, 'Actually I do.' He shook his head disapprovingly and then told her: 'Minnie here does the best dogs this side of the river. I'll take mine with the works.'

Minnie opened up the bun and started ladling onions and then squirting ketchup and mustard on top of the sausage.

'I'll have the same,' said Lil. Minnie continued to layer up Abe's hot dog with mayonnaise, chilli sauce and pickles. 'On reflection, hold the works. Just give me onions and ketchup.'

'Coming up.' Minnie winked at her again.

'So . . . ?' The detective leant in closer and dropped his voice. 'What do you hear?'

Minnie's gaze flitted around before handing

Lil a hot dog in a serviette. She replied in a whisper, 'Those fires have got everyone spooked.'

Abe narrowed his eyes and took the hot dog he was offered. 'OK, Minnie, I'll bite. What have you heard?'

Minnie shrugged. 'Take a look at this.' She pulled a copy of the *Klaxon* out from beneath a bag of finger rolls, licked her thumb and turned to the second page. She read the article out loud.

Death of Prison Doctor is "Unexplainable"

'Yesterday evening Dr Hans Carvel burnt to death while locked in his office on the Secure Wing for the Criminally Insane at Fellgate Prison.

'Several members of prison staff are willing to testify that due to the extreme security conditions on the ward the doctor was not only under guard at all times but his office door was double-locked from the

inside. Police have no CCTV inside the room, though there are plenty of cameras surrounding it, and there was no sign of an intruder. It was reported to have been a suicide but the Klaxon *can reveal that expert investigators have been unable to ascertain the source of the fire.'*

'It's an unusual way to do yourself in,' Abe mused.

'Furthermore, police photographs taken at the scene reveal deep and frantic nail marks on the inside of the wooden door. The scratches contain ingrained traces of soot suggesting they were made during the fire and not before it.'

'So, the Firebug strikes again?' Abe said, but he didn't look convinced. 'Except we all know that the other victims all had a past – they were ex-mobsters.'

Lil pulled out a pencil and chewed on the

end of it. 'Maybe there's another connection?'

Minnie shrugged. 'If it's the Firebug, then he's one clever so-and-so. The door was locked from the inside and it was under guard. It would have been impossible for anyone to get in without being seen.'

'Not impossible,' Nedly murmured darkly.

'You would have thought this city was too damp to burn,' muttered Abe.

Minnie squinted at the ex-police detective. 'So, what's all the interest? Are you on the case?'

'You know me, Minnie,' Abe replied. 'I'm just curious.'

'Well, good luck! Someone's got to stop him. You know, the police – they aren't even investigating. Some of the guys were down here the other day; off the record they say it looks like murder but they've got nothing to go on. I heard them: "No forensics, no witnesses." Whoever it was, they came and went like a ghost.'

Lil choked on a piece of onion. She looked at Nedly.

'Don't look at me!' he said.

Minnie pulled her coat round her and looked over her shoulder again. 'And that's not all that's happening over at the Needle. It might be something, it might be nothing, but the new doctor, down there at the Secure Wing, who's just took over from the dead one, he's got the place locked down – saying there's an outbreak of some kind of sickness there. One of the inmates has already died, but no one is saying who.' Minnie wrinkled her nose and grunted. 'Good riddance, some say. One less prisoner to pay for.'

Abe frowned. 'They've got a new doc in post already? That's fast work. Sounds like someone was waiting in the wings, a motive for a copycat maybe. You think it's connected?'

Lil saw a glimmer of something in Abe's eyes that sharpened his gaze, a faint suggestion of his former steely glare.

Minnie gave an offhand snort. 'Who knows?' She stopped flipping onions and gave the detective this X-ray-eye look. 'One more thing, hot off the press, so to speak.' She took a long sweep of the street on either side and then lowered her voice to an almost-whisper. 'Rumour has it the *Klaxon* is about to break a big story. It's all hush-hush but the word is they've got their hands on some incriminating materials: official documents, ledgers, that kind of thing.' She leant in conspiratorially. 'Enough to bring down the Mayor's Office.'

Abe rubbed his jaw with the prosthetic hand. 'The last time anyone took a shot at City Hall, it was McNair.'

Minnie frowned gravely. 'And we all know how that ended.'

They nodded silently at each other and then Lil gulped, breaking the spell. Abe passed her his hot dog while he fumbled in his pocket for some change.

Minnie shrugged and looked at the money. 'You're a bit short there, Detective. Have you got another five?'

Two police officers swaggered up to the stand. One male, one female. They both wore standard-

194

issue clear shower caps that stretched over their hats to protect them from the rain. All Peligan City police wore them all the time.

The male one flashed them a smile. 'Well, look who it is. *Ex*-police detective Absolom Mandrel.'

Abe smiled back with wary politeness, still rummaging in his pocket to find the extra five to pay Minnie.

'I just came to get a hot dog,' he said in a way that sounded like 'I'm not looking for any trouble'. The money was eluding him. Lil reached into her pockets and started pulling out some coins.

Abe's cheeks began colouring. 'No, kiddo, forget it. I said I'd treat you, didn't I?'

Lil watched as he pulled out fluff and old receipts and a small note, which caught the wind and flew away.

'You can both forget it,' Minnie said obligingly. 'It's on me – for old times.'

Abe looked like he was going to refuse but then, his shoulders slumped in defeat, he gave

Minnie a smile of weary gratitude. 'Thanks.' He took the hot dog back from Lil. 'I'll see you around, Minnie.'

They were only ten feet away when the male officer's voice caught up with him.

'He's the old-timer that got washed up on the Lucan Road Mob case. They retired him early and good job too – he was a drunk. Still is, by the look of him.'

Abe stopped in his tracks. He passed his hot dog to Lil again and then pulled off his prosthetic hand. The officers at the hot dog stand had stopped talking. It seemed to Lil as though the streets had fallen silent, holding their breath the same way she was. Abe picked through the Swiss Army attachments and pulled out a flat metal object shaped like a crab's claw.

'What are you going to do?' Lil whispered. She looked back at the hot dog stand. The officers were watching Abe's back. No one moved.

'Eat my hot dog, that's what.' He held out his hand for the bun, placed it in the pincer and turned a screw to tighten the grip.

196

'Come on, we've got work to do.'

Lil ran after him. Nedly stayed behind.

A moment later the police officer yelped and jumped, dropping his hot dog in the overflowing gutter.

His partner frowned at him. 'What is wrong with you?'

The man looked around him fearfully, his heart still galloping. 'I don't know, I just . . . I mean, I thought I just . . . never mind. I just got a bad feeling.'

Chapter 15

Pop Goes the Weasel

This was the plan: Abe would leave Lil and, unbeknownst to him, Nedly in the lobby of the Mingo while he went up to his rooms to look for something he could pawn for petrol money so that the Zodiac could make the trip to the Hawks Memorial Orphanage out at Bun Hill. While Abe checked some facts with the caretaker, Mr Kolchak, Lil was going to interview the kids who had known Ned Stubbs to see if any of them remembered anything about the night he went missing.

But plans change: while Lil and Nedly were waiting in the dimly lit lobby, perched on the corners of a mangy-looking velveteen settee pockmarked with cigarette burns and smelling faintly of old dog fur, the front door was kicked open so hard it hit the wall and rebounded on the person in the doorway.

Craig Weasel recovered quickly from the blow and stood silhouetted on the threshold, like the sheriff in the last chance saloon. He was slickly dressed in an aubergine suit, his gelled ponytail protruding stiffly from the back of his head like a cherry stalk.

'What's *he* doing *here*?' Lil dropped quickly out of sight and scuttled behind the settee. Keeping low, she crawled to the end of it and peered out from between the dusty leaves of a plastic Swiss cheese plant.

Weasel strode up to the glass phone booth in the corner of the lobby and unhooked the receiver. He dialled a number and then waited, grinding his teeth impatiently. Finally someone answered.

'I'm here now, sir,' he replied, silky smooth. 'If he's poking around, he must have got a sniff of something. Either him or that kid we picked up on the CCTV . . . Yeah, the one with the ears.'

Lil crawled back out of sight. 'What does that even mean?' she hissed to Nedly, the colour rising in her cheeks. 'Everyone has ears.'

Nedly shot her a glance. 'How do you know he's talking about you?'

Lil scowled while she tried to think of a good response. 'My signature look is the yellow mac – why didn't he say, the one with the yellow mac?' She untucked her hair and smoothed it over her ears.

'Either way,' Weasel continued into the receiver, 'if he's looking for trouble he's found it.' He fell silent as Abe's distinctive tread sounded on the staircase: heavy-footed, landing on each step like he was punishing it for something.

'*Ex*-Detective Mandrel,' the mayor's bodyguard said smoothly, hanging up the receiver with a soft click. 'I was just coming to see you.'

Lil snuck a glance to see Abe leaning on the banister; he flicked the brim of his hat so it tilted back on his head. 'Who are you?'

'Aha ha ha!' Craig Weasel laughed mirthlessly, clearly peeved that Mandrel didn't know who he was. 'It seems like you and your jug-eared sidekick have been making a nuisance of yourselves at City Hall.'

Abe walked slowly down the last of the steps and into the lobby.

'Look, pal, I don't know who you are or what you're talking about, so why don't you beat it before I get the wrong idea?'

Weasel seemed pleased with the way things were turning out. 'Why don't you make me, old man?' he said, dangling the challenge.

Abe wasn't biting. 'Get lost,' he growled, taking another step forward.

'Oh, I'll get lost all right . . .' Weasel replied in an oily voice.

'Good.' Abe made to walk by but when they levelled Weasel gave him a shove.

'Hey!' Lil protested, standing up. Both men

were distracted by her sudden appearance but Weasel recovered first. Abe turned back just in time to get a foot in the chops as Weasel delivered a sudden roundhouse kick.

'What the . . . ?' Abe reeled back clutching his jaw and tripped over the Swiss cheese plant. He flailed around on the floor like a beetle on his back until Lil darted forward to help him to his feet.

Abe shook his head to clear it, felt his jaw gingerly and then peeled off his mac. He kept his eyes fixed on the younger man, sizing him up as he tossed Lil his hat.

'Are you going to frighten me to death with a striptease, Mandrel?' Weasel sniggered. He was dancing on the spot like a boxer, his hands raised and held flat like he was about to do some serious karate.

Abe pushed up his sleeves. 'Stay back, kid,' he ordered Lil with a flick of his head.

Lil hurried out of range to her spot behind the settee. She crouched there with just her head visible over the back of it. Nedly lurked awkwardly at the edge of the action.

Craig Weasel grabbed his own shirt with both hands and ripped it apart, exposing a purple silk kimono tied with a black sash. He kicked off his shoes, and his trousers slid down to reveal matching purple silk bottoms.

'Yah!' winced Lil. 'Who wears a karate outfit under his normal clothes?'

'A man who is prepared for a fight!' cried Weasel, drawing a pair of black-handled nunchucks out of the pile of discarded clothes.

'What the . . . ?' Abe said again.

'Give it up, old man.' Weasel spun the chain around at high speed in a Web of Death; Lil could see his shark-like grin through the silver and black blur. He switched moves to pass the nunchucks over his shoulders, retrieving them from behind his elbows like some crazy dance routine. A smug expression clung to his face; his hair had started to come free of its ponytail and hung in crispy strings.

Abe tucked in his chin and put up his fist ready to box. When Weasel saw him his serious fighting face erupted in a gale of laughter. 'Ah,' he sighed, wiping the tears from his eyes. 'Seriously? OK, let's do it.'

He passed the nunchucks from hand to hand, spinning the chain in a figure of eight. Abe watched, bewildered; a couple of times he tentatively jabbed in with his left hand but the wooden handle rapped his knuckles hard and he withdrew.

'Come on, Abe!' Lil shouted. She looked around for something to throw him – something that would get in the nunchucks' way. There was a telephone directory in the phone booth . . . Lil scrambled around to it and she lobbed the fat book straight at Weasel's back.

It knocked him slightly off balance for a second and he stumbled forward; the nunchucks went slack and Abe drove him back with a flat rubber uppercut to the chin followed by a left hook. He seemed almost as surprised as Weasel to have got a punch in.

Then it all started to go wrong. Pleasantly startled by the effectiveness of his first two slugs, Abe delivered a quick volley of punches to Weasel's rock-solid belly with no noticeable effect. Weasel snagged Abe by his shirt and spun him, then he grabbed the nunchucks by both handles and clamped them round Abe's neck like a giant nutcracker.

He squeezed the handles closer together and the more he squeezed, the purpler Abe's face grew, and the more his eyes bulged.

'Let him go!' shouted Lil, running at Weasel. She grabbed his hand and tried to prise the fingers away from the nunchucks.

'He's freakishly strong,' she gasped, trying to loosen the vice-like grip.

Lil bit down on a knuckle bone. Weasel yelped and pulled his hand away – the chain loosened for a moment and Abe choked back a breath. He managed to get his fingers under it before Weasel pinched the handles even tighter as he transferred them to one hand – and with the other he grabbed Lil by the scruff of her coat

205

and lifted her off the ground. He tucked her head under his arm and let her dangle in a headlock.

'Melp!' Her cry was muffled by silk and Weasel's armpit. 'Melp!'

'Take your hands off her!' Abe wheezed, trying to get a grip on Weasel's slippery kimono.

'There's no one left to help you, shortie,' Weasel sneered and tightened his grip.

Lil kicked him hard on the shin.

The low lights in the lobby flickered and went out. The telephone in the booth started ringing and the front door juddered. Weasel turned quickly this way and that, dragging his captives with him. The light came on again and straight away the bulb overhead blew, sprinkling Weasel with fine, hot glass.

'This place is a dump!' he cursed. 'Come on, someone wants to see you.' He started walking towards the door, Abe and Lil in tow.

Lil saw Nedly rush at Weasel, shouting. Then, with a pop, he vanished. Weasel's face drained of all colour. He shivered dramatically and then started twitching. His arms went limp and both

Abe and Lil dropped to the floor, clutching their necks. Abe was the first to get to his feet. Lil scrambled up a second later and grabbed a chair, holding it in front of her like a shield.

Craig Weasel was acting very strangely; he was looking at his hands as if he'd never seen them before, and he was turning his head mechanically as though he was about to break into a robotic dance.

Abe frowned. He raised his fist again ready to fight but when Weasel didn't respond in kind he dropped it again. Weasel was prancing, raising each leg like a puppet on tangled strings. Lil lowered her chair.

'What are you playing at?' Abe growled at him.

Weasel didn't seem to know. His eyes had a glazed look and his movements were jerky as if he wasn't in control of his body. Plus, he seemed to have forgotten how to use the nunchucks. He swung them back and forth like a whip, occasionally cracking himself on the head with one end.

Lil and Abe stood watching, transfixed, and then Weasel turned to them with a curious expression, grabbed his own throat as though he was being strangled and screamed: 'RUN!!!'

Lil made a grab for Abe; she clasped his prosthetic hand and pulled it right off. Flustered, she shoved it back at him and shouted: 'Come on!'

Abe snatched his hat and mac off the settee and they hurled themselves down the front steps and into the street. Without warning Nedly burst through the wall beside them and sped past yelling: 'Run!' Lil watched him tear off round the corner and then picked up speed.

They ran four blocks before they were sure that Craig Weasel wasn't following. Abe found a bench and collapsed there with his head between his legs. He was huffing and puffing; one button of his shirt had come off and his tie was loose and over one shoulder. Lil was bent over double trying to get her breath back. Nedly stood apart – he looked both terrified and exhilarated.

'You – were – a-mazing!' Lil gasped at Nedly between breaths. 'How did you do that?'

'Thanks,' Abe wheezed bashfully. The sweat was soaking through his shirt and his face was pale. 'I guess I've still got a few moves.'

Lil spluttered out a laugh, which she expertly turned into a cough. She winked at Nedly who shrugged back at her. 'It just happened,' he said, blushing grey and looking at his shoes.

Abe fanned himself with his trilby. 'That guy –'

'Weasel,' Lil inserted.

'Indeed,' Abe agreed. 'That *weasel* was as crazy as a coconut.'

'No, I mean his name is Weasel. He's the mayor's bodyguard. He said you'd been looking for trouble at up at City Hall.'

Abe snorted. 'I was just chewing the fat with the guy on the desk about McConkey getting marshmallowed. Come to think of it, that Weasel character was in the lift with the mayor when he came down to the lobby, but he didn't stick around. The mayor took one step out of the lift, and then got in it again and went back up.'

'Why do you think that was?'

'I figured he'd forgotten something.' Abe wiped the sweat off his face with his handkerchief. 'But you know there is something about Mayor Dean. The way he looked at me, it was clear he didn't like what he saw.'

Lil scratched her nose thoughtfully. 'Remember those stolen files Minnie was talking about, the ones the *Klaxon* are going to use against the Mayor's Office? Maybe Weasel thinks you had something to do with that.'

'I don't know but somehow I've tugged a thread on a spider's web, and now that ginger tarantula is twitching to get at me.' He pulled at a tear in the pocket of his rumpled suit jacket. 'This was my best suit.' He dropped his gaze down to his shoes.

'Look, kid, it's not safe for you to be around me right now. I need to stay low until things cool off while I work out what all this means. I'm going to have a lie-down in a dark room, maybe a drink or two.'

Lil furrowed her brow. 'But the orphanage . . . ?'

'For all I know Weasel was intending to fit us with a couple of pairs of concrete galoshes and take us swimming in the Kowpye. How do you think I'd look your mother in the eye if I got you killed, eh? Think about it, she'd never forgive me.' He sank his chin into his collar.

Lil persisted. 'The orphanage, *you said* . . .'

'We'll go another time. Get yourself home, kid. Keep out of trouble until I figure this out.' He patted his pockets and then grimaced. 'I'd give you some money for the bus home but I don't have any.'

'Forget it,' said Lil. She was tired of people handing her money for the bus when what they meant was *get lost*.

They watched the detective limp off into the distance.

'So, is Abe off my case again now?' Nedly asked despondently.

Lil gave him a rueful smile. 'Don't worry – I'm still on the case, and *I* never give up.'

Chapter 16

Babyface Sings

The Hawks Memorial Orphanage was on the outskirts of town. As Lil pedalled her bike away from the smog towards the city limits the sky brightened from sardine-grey to oyster-white and the rain turned to a soft mizzle.

Her pockets were loaded with freshly purchased bribes: toffees and fruit chews mostly, from the shop on the corner. Nedly, who was thankfully entirely weightless, was perched on the handlebars so she had to crane her neck round him to see the road. She wore fingerless gloves, a heavy Mexican poncho and a balaclava against the creeping chill of being so close to him, but as the road out of Peligan was mostly uphill she was feeling pretty hot and bothered by the time they arrived.

At the top of Bun Hill they wobbled to a stop. Lil dumped her bike on an overgrown lawn and peeled off the balaclava.

The orphanage was a large square building, three stories high and eight windows across. There were bright curtains in the windows, but the front door was peeling paint and ivy had a strangle-hold on the drainpipes.

Lil caught sight of a small round face, as pale and bald as the moon, against the darkness of an upstairs window. The little boy was watching her intently but when she raised a hand to wave at him he backed away from the glass until he was out of sight.

'Babyface,' Nedly murmured and then he shuddered violently.

'You knew him?'

Nedly nodded and his eyes clouded over until they were almost black.

'OK,' said Lil. 'Let's go rattle his cage a bit.'

'Go easy on him. He's only six.' Nedly faltered. 'No . . . he would be seven now, I suppose.'

'Well, if he knows something he's going to have to spill it.' She squinted up at the now empty window. 'We need a break if we're going to crack this case.' She started down the path but Nedly hung back. 'Don't be getting all sentimental on me,' Lil told him. 'We've got to squeeze this kid for answers. You need to act like a professional.' She gave him a stern look. 'You might have to put the frighteners on him.'

She knocked on the door and waited. After what seemed like almost too long the door opened and the orphanage caretaker, Mr Kolchak, stood on the threshold, wearing a blue denim apron plastered with flour and his shirt sleeves rolled up to the elbows. His eyes squinted out beneath white-tufted brows.

'Hello,' said Lil, giving him a trustworthy smile. 'My name is Lil. I'm an associate of Abe Mandrel P.I., the detective who's working your case. He sent me in to interrogate some of the orphans. I mean, talk to them – about Ned Stubbs.'

'I haven't seen Mandrel for a long time,' Mr Kolchak mused. 'He always maintained that young Ned ran away, of course,' he added ruefully, 'but I'm relieved to hear he's still looking. I almost thought he'd given up on us.' Lil winced inwardly. 'Who do you want to talk to?'

Lil pulled out her reporter's notebook in a let's-get-down-to-business-like way and extracted the pencil. She pointed it at the top of the building. 'Third floor, fourth window from the left. I want to talk to the one they call Babyface.'

'That's Clark's room,' Mr Kolchak told her with a frown. 'Some of the kids do call him Babyface, but I happen to think that's a bit unkind.'

Lil reddened and cast an annoyed look at Nedly.

'Sorry,' he shrugged. 'The name just stuck.'

They cornered the boy in his tiny bedroom. The cheerful blue paint had bubbled where damp patches spread across the plaster, and the ceiling bowed in the corner where the roof was leaking. A small bed with a cloud-pattered coverlet stood in the corner with a toy box at the end of it. Sitting beside the toy box, reading a book about trains, was Babyface Kennedy, his bald head blooming out of his thick turtleneck jumper like a light bulb.

Mr Kolchak cleared his throat. 'Ahem. Clark, I've got someone here to see you.' Babyface turned and glanced up at him. 'Her name is Lil and she'd like to ask you some questions about young Ned.'

Lil stepped out from behind the old man with a wolfish grin.

'Pleased to meet you, Clark,' she said. 'Thanks, Mr Kolchak. I can take it from here.'

Nedly slipped in through the open door and the afternoon light turned grey. Babyface got the creeps straight away; his eyes darted fearfully between the dark corners of the room and he started trembling.

'Don't be nervous, Clark.' Mr Kolchak nodded encouragingly at him. 'I'll just be downstairs if you need me.' He gave Lil a melancholy smile and then shuffled out onto the landing and creaked down the wooden stairs and out of earshot.

Lil stared at the little boy. His huge brown eyes glistened above his chapped red cheeks and small chin, and his teeth were small and widely spaced, but most striking of all was his head; it was completely bald and looked bluish-white in the stark attic light.

'So, that's why they call you Babyface,' she said.

'Lil!' Nedly hissed angrily at her as a red blush crept up from the little boy's collar and over his neck. He touched a small hand to his hairless scalp and then unhooked a woollen hat from the bedpost and slipped it on.

'How do you know they call me that?' he asked.

'There's a lot that I know,' Lil replied. She pulled out a roll of Cherry Drops from her mac pocket and offered him one. A smile broke over his face and he held out a pink-fingered paw to take it.

'Not so fast,' Lil warned, holding it out of reach. Babyface looked covetously at the sweets and then back at Lil.

Helping herself to a dusty-looking leather pouffe, Lil sat down opposite the little boy while Nedly stood in a corner behind him, half out of focus, a shadow amongst shadows.

Babyface shrank into his jumper.

'I'm not looking for any trouble,' Lil assured him. 'I just need some answers. As soon as I saw you at that window, I thought, that kid knows something.'

Babyface employed the most effective response he could muster. He turned down his mouth, stuck out his bottom lip and said nothing.

'Not talking, eh?' Lil gave Nedly a barely

perceptible nod that meant, *OK, give him the creeps.*

Nedly took a reluctant step forward. Babyface's head whipped round; he searched the dark but seemingly empty corner behind him and ran a nervous finger round the collar of his turtleneck to loosen it.

Lil leant towards him with a not-so-friendly smile. 'No reason to get twitchy, Babyface. It's just you and me here.'

She fixed the little boy with her Penetrating Squint. 'OK,' she said. 'Let's hear it. I want to know what happened the night Ned Stubbs went missing.'

Lil helped herself to a couple of Babyface's Jelly Tots from a wrinkled and yellowing bag by the toy box, throwing one up in the air and catching it in her mouth. It had been several months since she'd learned how to do that without choking and this was the first time she had been able to use it.

Babyface looked more disappointed than impressed. 'I was saving those,' he whined.

Lil pulled a face. 'No kidding. That one tasted of earwax. How old are they?'

Babyface shrugged. 'Mr Kolchak bought them for me after Ned . . . to cheer me up.' His large eyes clouded over and started to rain fat tears that soaked his eyelashes and trickled down his cheeks.

Lil looked at her shoes. It was a dirty job all right, but someone had to do it.

'Dry your eyes, kiddo,' she told him. 'Your tears won't wash with me. Now, you tell me what happened the night Ned disappeared or I'll eat the whole bag.'

Babyface hung his bald head down and stared at his feet. He wasn't wearing any shoes and she could see a tiny pink toe poking out of a hole in his sock. 'All right, I'll talk.' With a quivering intake of breath he began: 'Ned went looking for Wool –'

Lil watched as Nedly's face grew pale and haunted-looking. '*Wool?*' he said. The faraway sound of his voice filled her with dread.

'Wool?' she queried Babyface. 'What did he want wool for?'

Her eyes darted back to Nedly, but he wasn't listening. The temperature in the room was turning Arctic and Lil could feel her pulse throbbing in her neck, while Nedly stood, staring into space and murmuring to himself as his mind tried to catch at the fragile wisps of memory. 'That was his name, he whispered. *Wool*, of course. It was a toy.' His head snapped up and he rushed towards Lil with an urgent and meaningful stare. 'A *missing* toy.'

Lil gave Nedly a tiny shrug of confusion, and subtly dodged round him to continue questioning Babyface. 'Can you describe it for me?'

Babyface shrugged. 'It's my woollen humpty.'

'I've no idea what that means,' Lil confessed. 'Can you draw me a picture?'

'You have a picture,' Nedly insisted.

'I really don't,' Lil mouthed back at him while the little boy fetched a crayon and a piece of paper from the toy box and, with his tongue curled out in concentration, began to draw a wobbly egg shape with chipolata arms and legs. He gave the figure round hollow eyes and a few strings of hair.

Lil stared at the picture for a moment, and then she rummaged in the pocket of her mac, drew out the crumpled Lost Toy poster from the bus station noticeboard and held it up alongside the one that Babyface had drawn.

'Is this yours?'

Babyface nodded sadly. 'Mr Kolchak put it up for me, but no one ever answered it.'

Lil raised an eyebrow at Nedly.

He nodded gravely in return. 'Wool is the face I saw, in my dream. It was there, when it happened.'

Tears began rolling down Babyface's still-blotchy cheeks again. 'They kidnapped him,' he sniffled. 'The older boys. They hid him so I couldn't find him.'

'*OK*,' Lil said, pulling her balaclava out of her pocket and handing it to him to wipe his eyes with. 'And this "humpty" thing was what Ned was looking for the night he went missing?'

Babyface nodded.

'And where exactly did he go to find this Wool character?'

Babyface looked closely at her like he was weighing up whether or not he should tell. He climbed to his feet, walked over to the window, pointed one finger out and spoke in a voice that was almost too quiet to hear. 'In there.'

Lil charted the line of his little red digit over the lane and across the fields to where the murky skyline was broken by a building. The sight of it made her blood run cold.

'The old asylum,' she whispered. Beside her Nedly shivered, then she shivered, then Babyface shivered. 'They say it's haunted.'

'It is.' Babyface's eyes quivered fearfully. 'Now Wool is there and Ned is there and neither of them has ever come back.'

'Has anyone checked it out?'

Babyface looked away, ashamed of himself. 'I'm too scared to go in.'

Lil reached out to ruffle his hat in a friendly

way but he evaded her hand. 'I didn't mean you, small fry. An adult, like Mr Kolchak.'

He shook his head miserably. 'We're not supposed to go in there. It's off-limits. I didn't want to get Ned into trouble.' His lip started to quake and he hung his head, looking wretched.

'It's too late for that, kid,' Lil muttered under her breath.

Nedly touched her lightly on the shoulder, sending a cold shudder through her bones. He gave her a look that meant, *He knows that, give him a break, he's only seven* – or something to that effect.

Lil frowned and patted down her pockets. She pulled out the tube of Cherry Drops again, plus some fruit chews and a bag of toffees, and stacked them in Babyface's outstretched hands. 'There you go, pal. These are nearly new. You can dump the Jelly Tots now.'

The little boy took them shyly. 'Toffees are my favourite,' he said as he opened up the packet and offered her one.

'Give mine to the old man,' suggested Lil. 'He looks like he could do with cheering up.'

Babyface nodded eagerly. 'Maybe you could stay for a bit?'

Lil chewed her lip, 'I'm sorry, Babyface. I've got things to do. I'll come again another time.'

The little boy tried to smile. 'OK,' he said, but he didn't sound too hopeful.

Lil watched him carefully sorting through the sweets, dividing them into two piles. 'I miss him,' he whispered, as though he was talking to himself.

Lil paused with her hand on the door knob. She glanced across at Nedly and caught the sad look on his face. 'He misses you too, kid.'

The road to Rorschach Asylum twisted through an overgrown thicket of buckthorn and gorse. A rusted metal sign arced over the driveway, above a tall cast-iron gate that was chained, padlocked shut and festooned with dented warning notices. The soot-dusted brick shell rose behind it like a reanimated corpse-face, decayed but still breathing. Lil held its gaze for an uneasy moment while the sky darkened around them and the wind picked up.

She propped her bike up against the gate and they started examining the criss-cross wire fence, looking for a way in.

'There!' She pointed at a hole, a tear at the bottom of the nearest post where the fence had been ripped away, leaving a flap edged with sharp metal barbs. 'There's a gap in the fence. We could climb through.'

A look of recognition dawned on Nedly and he rubbed at the back of his hand where the thin red welt still looked like a fresh scratch. 'That wire is sharp.'

'So this really is the place.' Lil glanced from the wound to Nedly with a serious expression. 'We've found it then, the beginning of the end.' They looked up and the burnt face of the asylum leered back down at them. 'I don't fancy going in there alone,' she said, shivering.

They both stood in awkward silence for a minute, while Lil tucked and untucked her hair and Nedly examined the cut on the back of his hand.

'Come on,' said Lil. 'We need backup. Let's go get him.'

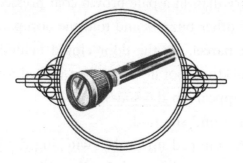

Chapter 17

Next on the List

Nobody was answering the buzzer for Hawaiian Island Suite Three; Lil had already pressed it three times, holding it down to a determined count of twenty on each go.

'Maybe he's gone out?' suggested Nedly. 'We could try the Nite Jar?'

Lil pondered it. 'Yeah, maybe.'

'Unless . . .' Nedly shuddered. 'You don't think Weasel came back and got him?'

Lil bit her lip. 'Nah, he's probably just asleep

up there.' She moved out of the way as a delivery man in a pale brown coat pressed one of the other buzzers and told the occupant she had a parcel. As the door closed behind him Lil stuck her foot in it and then waited for him to disappear up the stairs.

'Come on,' she said.

They tramped upwards, switching the lights on as they reached each landing. Lil sensed an unusual level of reluctance in Nedly. He was lagging behind.

'You know, it's OK if you don't want to come with us to Rorschach. I mean, I understand, given the situation with you being . . . d-different now. If we do find anything you . . . you might not want to see it.'

The lights on the staircase between floors four and five flickered and somewhere in a far-off room a tiny cat's-collar bell tinkled urgently. 'We might find . . . me. My body, I mean,' Nedly said flatly. 'I know.'

'But I'll be there with you,' said Lil. 'Whatever happens, OK?'

There was no answer. Nedly had stopped midway down the stairs; he was standing very still. 'OK?' she said again.

He held up a hand as if to say, *Be quiet a minute,* then he whispered. 'Did you hear that?'

She listened and then shook her head. 'Hear what?'

'Someone laughing.'

Lil shrugged. 'I know it's an unusual sound in this place but –'

'No, it's not like that. It wasn't a nice laugh.' A doomed look came into his eyes. 'I've heard it before somewhere.'

'When you say "somewhere" . . .'

'Somewhere bad.'

A chill snaked up Lil's spine.

Nedly's expression was pale and pinched. 'Something's wrong.'

The air felt too still. They crept onwards and the lights went off just before they reached the landing as usual, but this time Lil's breath plumed out in the darkness, a cloud of mist.

They could hear the sound of doors banging upstairs.

Fear sent a rush of adrenalin through her veins. 'Come on!' she shouted, and they started running. She hit the next switch as they reached the sixth-floor landing and then launched herself back off the wall and towards the last flight of stairs, but Nedly suddenly stopped in his tracks and she nearly ran through him. He took a step backwards, pinning himself to the sticky wallpaper, his eyes stretched wide in his thin white face as they tracked something moving past.

A curl of sharp cold air wound round Lil, stinging her cheeks like a burn. Fear tightened its grip, squeezing the breath out of her lungs.

'Nedly? What are you doing?' She stepped into his sightline. 'Cut it out, you're giving me the creeps.'

'Nedly!' she yelled, glaring at him even as he looked past her, transfixed by something on the stairs. 'Come on! We don't have time for this.'

Nedly suddenly snapped out of it. He panic-

232

blinked a few times then said: 'You're right.'

Lil smelt the smoke before she saw it creeping towards them from the seventh-floor landing. The corridor ahead was fuzzy with it. The lights went off again and Lil stumbled. Gasping for breath, she picked herself up, patting down the walls to locate the light switch.

She found it in time to see Nedly running off ahead, unaffected by the smoke. When he reached the seventh floor he shot arrow-straight and head first through the wall into Abe's rooms. Lil made it to the top of the stairs a few moments later and tried the door. The handle was hot to the touch and she could see a thin veil of black smoke spreading from the gap under the door. She lurched back to the hallway, her sweatshirt over her nose and mouth and, following her mum's example, but not her advice, elbowed the glass box at the top of the stairs to set off the fire alarm.

Nothing happened.

She furiously cursed the landlord and then sucked in a lungful of fumy air and half screamed, half choked out the word: 'FIRE!'

With a noise like a cork popping Nedly shot back through the wall. 'I can't wake him!' he yelled.

Lil picked up a fire extinguisher.

'Do you know how to use one of those?'

'Yes,' she said and hurled it at the door to the Hawaiian Island Suite. The lock splintered and the door swung open. Lil leapt aside as a giant fiery breath was exhaled into the corridor.

The room was ablaze. Blue flames were running over the photos on the wall and spreading to the curtains, which lit up like touchpaper. The linoleum was blistering and curling at the edges. The settee had burst into a black and gold fireball and the boxes of files were smouldering, splitting open and spilling papers onto the floor where they caught light and were blown around by the gusts of hot air, igniting everything they came into contact with.

Lil stood in the doorway watching it as though hypnotised. The heat in there must have been unbearable but Abe didn't stir. She could see him silhouetted at the breakfast bar, slumped over the counter next to a bottle and an empty glass. Flames were licking at the rug by his feet, and then the smoke hit the back of her throat and she began to choke; the heat on her skin was searing. She held up an arm to cover her face.

'Go back!' shouted Nedly. 'It's too hot. I'll get him.' He looked at Lil. It was a look that said: *I promise.*

Lil stepped back into the corridor. She watched Nedly running frantically, knocking pots and pans off the rack in the kitchenette, sending books flying from the shelves like kamikaze pilots dive-bombing the lino. He was desperately trying to make enough noise to be heard over the roar of the flames but Abe wasn't moving. She ran to the corridor to look down the stairs to see if help had arrived but there was no one in sight. She pulled her mac over her head and stepped towards the room but as soon as she neared the door it began to soften and Lil realised it would melt.

The room was filling with a fog of noxious smoke. Lil could only just make out Nedly standing over Abe amongst the growing flames. He was flickering, only the whites of his eyes standing out in the black and orange inferno. He seemed to suck in a breath so huge that his whole body curled with the effort, and then he released it with a terrifying scream, full force, right into Abe's ear.

Abe woke with a start, fell back off his stool and onto the floor, where he came face to face with a carpet of luminous flames. He dragged himself to his feet, his eyes wide with panic. Coughing, bewildered, he gasped for breath and immediately started choking on the smoke. His good hand grabbed at his chest, trying to loosen his tie. He looked at the door where Lil stood waving her arms madly. She shouted his name above the heat, the roar of flames, and the din of the alarm bell, which had finally sounded on another floor.

'ABE!!!!' This way!'

As the detective stumbled towards her the

edge of his mac caught fire. He staggered through the door and onto his knees just as the cooker exploded, blowing the oven door off its hinges.

Leaning heavily on Lil and wheezing all the way down they made it to the sixth-floor landing, and then the sprinkler system came on.

Abe sat on the edge of the pavement with his feet in the gutter. His face was smudged grey with soot and his eyes were even more red-rimmed than normal. Curls of smoke were coming off his singed jacket and the thin rubber soles of his shoes had melted. He took his hat off and patted the bit that was still smouldering – beneath it his hair now had a streak of pure white.

'The fire crew said I was lucky to get out of there alive. I've got to make my way over to the hospital to get checked over, but all things considered . . .' His hand was shaking as he reached for his hipflask and then he looked at it grimly and chucked it over his shoulder into a pile of bin bags by the hotel steps. 'I guess you saved my life there, kid.' His bottom lip was trembling. Lil couldn't stand to look at it; a lump had risen in her own throat.

'It was the darnedest thing,' he continued. 'I've never been so scared . . . I was feeling a bit shaky,' he confessed, 'after the Weasel incident, but it was more than that; something didn't seem right. The radio kept coming on full volume, but it was just static, and then the heating went off and, well, that has been on the blink for days anyway. Maybe it was nothing. I don't know. It doesn't make any sense now. Maybe I'm just getting old.' He shook his head despairingly.

'Do you think it was Weasel?'

'The fire chief said it was probably some electrical fault. Just an unlucky accident.'

'An accident: that was what they said about the nurse that got killed at the hospital,' said Lil. 'And the security guard whose car blew up.'

'It wasn't an accident, and it wasn't Weasel,' said Nedly. 'I saw someone, someone on the stairs. They were laughing, and then they saw me, and they stopped.'

Lil frowned at Nedly, then she gave Abe a hearty pat on the shoulder and a puff of smoke rose into the air.

'Back in a tick,' she told him.

Lil stood scanning the menu through the steamed-up window of the Kam Moon Special Noodle Bar. Without looking at Nedly she murmured, 'Someone *saw you*?'

'He just passed us on the sixth-floor landing. You couldn't have missed him. He had blonde hair and his chin was scarred pink right down to his neck. Lil, you must have seen him; he walked right by you.'

Lil remembered the shiver she'd felt on the landing. 'No, I didn't see him, Nedly.'

'He walked right by you.'

'I didn't see him, OK!' she snapped, and then turned and looked straight at him. 'But he *saw*

you.' She frowned. 'What does that mean?'

'I think it means he's like me,' said Nedly.
'The Firebug is a ghost.'

Chapter 18

The Matron Only Knocks Once

Lil cut a lonely figure in the corridor of Peligan City Hospital, sitting on a chair with torn covers and foam bursting out of the seams. She had told the hospital administrator that Abe was her father so they let her stay with him, but they had insisted on calling her mother in anyway. They said she needed a responsible adult to take her home and Mandrel wasn't in any fit state. So now Lil was waiting, sipping stewed tea from a polystyrene cup and trying not to breathe in the smell that haunts all hospitals: disinfectant and boiled carrots.

She hadn't seen Nedly since they left the Mingo. His encounter with the apparition on the stairwell had disturbed him all right; he had said it was someone like him, a ghost. Only, this ghost bothered Lil because it *wasn't* like him; this ghost could do all sorts of things that Nedly couldn't, and this ghost had tried to kill someone – probably had killed people already. As far as Lil could see, the Firebug ghost was a very dangerous kettle of fish indeed, and he had seen Nedly, and now Nedly was alone, and who knew where?

Lil's mum arrived in an uncharacteristically animated state: breathless, with wild eyes and excitable hair.

'Thank the stars you're all right,' she gasped, spinning Lil round and checking her over. Her gaze flitted from her blackened face and dusty hair to her once bright yellow mac now grey with soot. 'You could have been burnt to a crisp!'

'I'm fine,' Lil insisted. 'Sorry they called you out of work.'

Naomi gave her a furious look for a moment, and then all the energy seemed to abandon her. She slumped down wearily on one of the half-eviscerated chairs beside Lil.

'I don't understand what you were doing there.'

'I was helping Abe with a case,' Lil said matter-of-factly.

'A case!' Naomi shook her head. 'How do you two even know each other?'

'I looked him up.' Lil shrugged. 'Anyway, I thought he was a friend of *yours*. I found a photograph of you two together. From the "good old days", the ones that you don't like to talk about,' she added ominously.

'Where exactly did you find the photograph?'

Lil shrugged guiltily. 'It was just stuck inside an old book.'

Naomi narrowed her eyes into slices. 'And where, exactly, did you find this book?'

'Somewhere in a box . . .' Lil mumbled, feeling hot. It felt like her mum had been working on a Penetrating Squint of her own so Lil was relieved when she got distracted by the sight of Matron Fry striding purposefully down the corridor towards them, carrying a pile of carefully folded but filthy-looking clothes in her arms. Matron Fry was heavy on the hips and her ash-blonde curls were flashed with grey. Her cheeks dimpled as she gave them a coral-coloured lipstick smile. 'Won't be long now. I'll tell him that you're waiting. That might cheer him up,' she added doubtfully.

She knocked sharply on the door across the hall and then flung it open. There followed the metallic whirr of a hospital curtain being yanked back, an affronted yelp and the scuffling sounds of someone tugging at bed sheets.

'Have you never heard of giving a person some privacy?' they heard Abe yell.

'Now, now, Mr Mandrel,' Matron Fry replied. 'There's no need to be shy. You haven't got anything I haven't seen a hundred times before. It's not my fault you decided to sit there in your underpants.'

'What did you expect me to wear?' Abe growled. 'All they left me with is this flimsy dress!'

'That's a hospital gown, Mr Mandrel. Everyone wears them here. Now, you have a couple of folks outside who have been asking after you. Can I let them in?'

'Can I get dressed first?'

Matron Fry stepped back out into the corridor. 'I'd like to have kept him in for some observation,' she explained to Lil's mum.

Lil heard Abe mutter something like, 'I bet you would!'

'But he is stubborn,' the matron continued. She smiled and shrugged her shoulders as if to say: *What can you do?*

As the door swung slowly shut behind her, Lil caught a glimpse of Abe sitting glumly on the edge of the bed, wrapped in a light blue sheet, his arms pale against his red and soot-darkened extremities. He was still wearing his battered trilby, now also singed at the edges, and for the first time Lil saw the brown-leather

246

strap that encircled his forearm and fastened his Swiss Army hand to the stump at the end of his wrist.

The door clicked shut and the matron lowered her voice. 'The truth is we can't keep him here if he doesn't want to stay, and we don't really have any free beds anyway so . . .' She tailed off, looking down the corridor with disappointment.

A moment later she gave another sharp knock on the door and peered in. She turned back to Lil and her mother. 'You can go in now.'

Abe stood by the bed in his blackened and ragged suit. When he saw who was waiting with Lil he looked taken aback.

'Naomi!' He just about breathed the word out.

'Abe. It's been a while,' Lil's mum said warmly.

'Good to see you.'

'You too, Abe. You look . . . well.' She flashed him a smile for old times' sake.

'I've been better.' Abe's cheeks coloured as he

hurriedly tucked in and smoothed down his shirt and straightened his tie. He took off his hat and ran a hand through his hair. 'I don't normally look as bad as this – it was the fire.'

Lil snorted.

The matron turned to Abe. 'We just need to get the paperwork signed off, and then you can go. You've suffered a bit of smoke inhalation and some minor burns, so you should take it easy for a couple of days.'

'I've had worse,' Abe said gruffly, reaching into his mac pocket and pulling out his prosthetic hand. He clicked it into place and gave it an appraising look. The fingertips had grown spoon-like where the heat of the fire melted them.

'Come on,' said Naomi. 'I'll give you a hand with the forms. Lil, could you get us a couple of coffees?'

Over at the nurse's station Abe furiously ticked his way through a pile of release forms. Naomi leant beside him, one elbow propped against the counter.

'Still making enemies, Abe?'

He snorted grimly. 'Someone wants me out of the picture. I seem to have ruffled some feathers with your friends down at City Hall.'

They watched Lil at the drinks machine emptying her pockets for change.

'Looks like you had help.' Naomi gave him a stern look. 'It seems my daughter has been spending a lot of time with you.'

'She's a good kid.'

'I know.'

Lil was flipping one of the coins in the air while the machine dispensed the coffee into polystyrene cups.

'Chip off the old block, eh?'

'She doesn't know about my past, Abe, and I'd prefer it if it stayed that way. I don't want her involved. We both know where it leads.' She acknowledged his nod with a single word. 'McNair.'

Abe said, 'Good luck with that. She's too much like you.'

'She doesn't think so.'

'You should tell her.' Abe finished the last form and tapped the pile together.

Naomi bit her bottom lip thoughtfully. 'It was good to see you again, Abe, but it has to end here. Whatever it is you're involved in, keep Lil out of it. She doesn't need any help getting into trouble; she's always managed that well enough by herself, and things are complicated at the moment so . . .'

At that moment Lil advanced on them with a 'Hey!' and two coffees. She took one look at Abe's grim hangdog face and asked, 'Are you OK?'

He winced, gave his chest a good punch and Lil a battered smile. 'Bit of heartburn, that's all.' His eyes went down to his half-melted old shoes.

'Thanks for the coffee.' Naomi downed hers in two and took control of the situation. She held out her arm. 'Have you got a ride home, Abe?'

Abe was rubbing the toe of his shoe on the back of his trouser leg, trying to magic up a shine. 'Don't worry about me,' he said. 'I'll be all right. I'm parked up below.'

'Well, I'll see you down to your car. Lil, meet me in the car park in five.'

Abe shuffled out, holding on to Naomi for support, like a bear leaning on a meerkat.

'They don't make them like that any more,' said the matron, as soon as they were out of earshot.

Lil pulled a face, but Matron Fry looked genuinely wistful. 'I remember him from way back in the day. I was just a junior nurse then and he was quite the hero. The Scourge of the Underworld, they called him. Oh, times are hard I know, but he's still got that look in his eye.' She smiled and the rosy apples of her cheeks pushed her eyes into twinkling blue crescents. 'He needs a good home-cooked meal. Does he have anyone special?'

'No,' Lil said, glancing down out of the window into the car park where she could see her mum and Abe talking under the light of a street lamp. 'He's been on his own a long while, I think. I look out for him, though,' she added protectively.

'I heard he hooked up with some hot-shot reporter way back when.'

'Maybe.' Lil shrugged. 'I don't know him that well.'

The matron gave her a wink. 'It would have been before your time, honey pie.'

Under the unforgiving orange lights of the Peligan City Hospital car park Abe struggled to get the door of the Zodiac open, and then had to grab at it quickly as whatever metallic thread it hung by seemed to snap and the door dropped by five inches.

Naomi watched him appraisingly. 'Do you think it's true – that you were the fourth intended victim of the Firebug Killer?'

'I hope not,' Abe said, grimly hoisting the door back into place. 'That would blow my theory right out of the window.' He eased himself into the driver's seat. 'I better go.' His throat was tight and his voice had grown thick. 'Take care of yourself, Naomi.'

He closed the door and pulled down the sunshield. The key dropped into his lap and then so did the shield itself. Abe threw it onto the back seat, and clenched and unclenched his jaw.

Naomi tapped on the window. 'Abe.' She hesitated while he stared fixedly ahead. 'About Lil . . .' But she was cut short when Lil caught up with them.

'Bye for now!' Lil called to Abe through the glass.

He started the car on the third attempt and pulled away. It cut out just before he exited the car park and then started again with a cloud of black smoke and disappeared from sight.

'Does he have somewhere to go?' asked Naomi.

Lil watched the 'No Exit' sign re-emerge from the engine smog. 'I hope so.'

As Lil's mum went to fetch the Datsun a sudden feeling of terrible dread swept over Lil. She shivered and slowly turned to see Nedly standing right behind her.

'There you are! Where did you go? I was getting worried; you shouldn't just disappear like that,' she scolded him and then noticed how wide and dark his eyes were looking. 'You OK?'

'I just needed some time to myself, to, you know, think about stuff.' He paused. 'By stuff, I mean *that ghost*. If only we could find out who he is . . .'

'Or was.' Lil pulled out her notepad and began flicking through the pages. 'You might be right. According to my notes the ghost you saw had a scar that ran from his mouth down to his neck. That's pretty distinctive. We might have a chance to track him down, find out why he's doing this.' She paused for a moment to chew on her pencil and then blew out a splinter of wood. 'But there was something else about him, you said – there was something familiar. You think you knew him?'

'No.' Nedly blanched. 'I just, maybe, I don't know. I could have seen his picture somewhere

I suppose, except . . . There's one other thing. He looked like he knew me too – when he saw me he stopped laughing and his face looked, I don't know, sad.'

'Maybe it was because you're a ghost too?'

'Yeah, maybe.' He looked off towards the visitor's car park; a plaintive whine sounded in the distance, heralding the approach of her mum's Datsun.

Lil sighed. 'Now what do we do? I mean, we know that the person who torched Abe's apartment is a ghost but I'll never be able to convince Abe he's being haunted. And we don't even know for sure that the ghost is the Firebug Killer, the one who's been going after the Lucan Road Mob and the doctor at the prison, though it would explain the lack of evidence and the near impossible nature of the crimes. It all fits, but Abe's never going to buy into it without some kind of proof.' She chewed off the end of her pencil and spat it on to the ground. 'You know, it would be so much easier if he could see you.'

'You're telling me!'

'If only there was some way.'

The Datsun's headlights appeared as Naomi Potkin turned out of the car park and began edging along the road, looking for Lil.

Nedly thought for a moment and then said, 'It's time.'

'To go?'

'To tell Abe, about me.'

Lil winced. 'I'm not sure that's a good idea.'

'He needs to know. Someone is after him, someone like me. We don't know why, but maybe he does. He's a target and we're withholding information. You have to tell him.'

'He won't believe me.'

'I'll convince him,' said Nedly with something close to an air of confidence. 'I've been working on some moves.'

Chapter 19

Milk and Five Sugars

The next morning the *Klaxon* ran the story on the front page:

Firebug Killer:
Failed Attempt on Fourth Victim?
Private Investigator Absolom 'Abe' Mandrel narrowly escaped a fiery death last night when his rooms at the Flamingo Hotel on Shoe Street were set ablaze. The official line from the PC Fire Department is that

this is just another case of faulty wiring and is not being viewed as suspicious.

Earlier this week three other victims – nurse Shirley Kreutz, security guard Antonio McConkey and prison doctor Hans Carvel – were all killed while alone and in confined spaces when the mysterious fires took hold.

But why was Mandrel targeted and who is behind these attacks? Blaming a lack of forensic evidence and witness testimonies, the authorities are reluctant to connect the dots and draw any conclusions in this case.

A whole day went by before Abe was allowed back into the remains of Hawaiian Island Suite Three. 'You didn't have to come with me, you know,' he grumbled at Lil. 'It's late and there's not much here worth saving. I could have taken care of it myself.' He plonked himself down on a burnt chair, which collapsed under his weight and then he sat on the floor, too angry to speak.

After a moment or two he stood up, feeling the seat of his trousers. 'Everything is dripping wet! Those crummy, two-bit sprinklers, they didn't put out the fire until all my stuff was destroyed anyway. Now anything that wasn't burnt to a crisp already is soaking. All my worldly goods . . .'

'Yeah.' Lil tried to keep some sincerity in her voice. 'And you had some really nice stuff too.' She looked at the charred remains of the Hawaiian sunset prints that were miraculously still hanging on the wall.

'And now I'm back to square one because first the doc got iced – well, consumed by fire – and now it looks like I'm on the Firebug Killer's list too, so it's not just the Lucan Road Mob he's after, and my theory is all wrong. The cases are connected in some other way, something I've missed, or maybe they're not connected at all. Now I'll never find Ramon LeTeef and bring him to justice.' He pulled up a warped metal bar stool and sat holding his head in his hands.

Lil gave his shoulder an encouraging pat. 'Yeah you will. I believe in you.'

Abe looked up at her with bloodshot eyes. 'Then you're a bigger schmuck than I am.' He let his head fall onto the sticky black surface of the counter. 'You've got me all wrong, kid. I'm just a nobody, living in the past. Does your mother know you're here?'

Lil ignored the question. 'Stop feeling sorry for yourself, Abe. You've got bigger fish to fry. Look, the *Klaxon* says you're the fourth intended victim of the Firebug Killer but I think they're wrong: you're actually the fifth. If my theory is correct, the Firebug Killer also tried to set fire to the mayor of Peligan City. Last Friday Mum came home smelling of burnt fleece. She said that there had been a fire at City Hall and she'd had to use the mayor's sheepskin jacket to put it out.'

Abe didn't move. She was talking to the top of his hat; the brim was folded back at the front and the band was barely clinging on to his head.

'So, he must have been right there where the fire was,' Lil continued. 'So, maybe the connection is between you, the nurse, Dr Carvel, the mayor and the exploded guard. Someone you have all wronged in the past, someone alive *or dead* who might have it in for you?'

Abe peeled his face off the counter; the soot had left a smear across his forehead. 'I used to be the Scourge of the Underworld, remember. Plenty of people alive and dead have it in for me – though I'm only really concerned with the "alive" ones.'

Lil looked him straight in the eye. 'That's where you're going wrong. It's the other kind you need to worry about.' She took a deep breath; it was time to come clean. Nedly gave her an encouraging nod. 'I've got a witness who can describe the Firebug, but there's something I need to tell you first. Come on, I better fix you a drink. You'll need one.'

They got the service lift down to the basement. Abe unlocked the first door they came to and fumbled for the light switch. 'Welcome to my new digs,' he said despondently.

The Ocean View Room had no windows. The breeze-block walls were painted deep blue and peppered with occasional orange blobs, and there was a stuffed toy octopus lounging across the pillow on the camp bed in the corner. A naked bulb hung on a long wire just above a blotchy-looking shaving mirror, and that was the only source of light apart from the rows of blue and green fairground bulbs that had been strung along the ceiling, giving the room an eerie underwater glow. It smelt of damp and there was a persistent dripping sound coming from some pipes that ran up the wall.

'I think Mr Teryaki made this room up,' grumbled Abe. 'I don't remember any Ocean View Room before. It looks like some kind of basement storage area. There are cupboards over there with cleaning supplies in and the other two suites on this floor are called the Laundry Room and the Utility Room. I can hear a furnace roaring all through the night and I have to use the bathroom on the next floor.'

'Well, it could be worse,' said Lil brightly, wondering if it could be, really.

She turned her back to examine one of the orange blobs, which turned out to be a hastily painted fish, and murmured to Nedly out of the corner of her mouth. 'Are you sure about this? It's nearly show time.'

He gulped nervously. 'I'm ready.'

Lil brewed up a couple of teas from a small travel kettle on a tray in the corner; she made one with two bags and then added three fingers of sugar.

'Abe, I think you should sit down.'

He unfolded a red-and-white-striped deck-chair, propped it up and then gingerly lowered himself into it until he was reclined at an uncomfortably laidback angle. Lil added another two fingers of sugar to his tea and gave it a brisk stir. 'Now, what I'm going to say will shock you. It might make you question the very meaning of your own existence and what comes after it.'

Abe snorted. Lil passed him the mug and then, cradling her own tea, she pulled up another deck-chair and sat down facing him.

'Do you remember you asked me once how I knew that the Ned Stubbs case was –' she lowered her voice – 'a *murder* investigation? Well, the reason I know is . . .' She paused. '*Because he told me.*'

'Who did?'

'Ned Stubbs told me.'

Abe let out a gruff snigger. 'Ned Stubbs told you he had been murdered? And you believed him?'

'I know this is hard for you to understand, Abe, but I can see him. The ghost of Ned Stubbs is here now, in this room.'

Abe took a sip of tea and then spat it straight out in a sticky brown spray.

'This must be a shock, I know, but . . .'

'Gah!' Abe interrupted. 'How much sugar is in this?'

'Just enough, I hope. Did you hear the bit about the ghost?'

'What ghost?'

Lil gritted her teeth impatiently. 'The ghost of Ned Stubbs.'

'You're saying that the ghost of Ned Stubbs appeared to you and told you he had been murdered and asked you to help him solve the case?'

'Yes!' Lil cried. 'That's exactly it. And what's more, he's here now.'

Abe knocked his prosthetic hand three times on the concrete floor. 'Whoooh! Is there anybody there?'

The fairground bulbs flickered, on and off and the air in the basement turned icy cool. The kettle on the stool began to rattle and then the whole tray flipped into the air and clattered to the floor. In the dim light Abe's face turned pale green. He took another gulp of his tea without even wincing and then patted down his pockets for a handkerchief and, not finding one, wiped the cold sweat from his brow with his tie.

It took him a moment to recover but as the

fear gradually drained away, it left behind something that looked a lot like disappointment. He shook his head at Lil.

'That's some trick, kid.'

'It's not a trick!' she protested. She gave Nedly the nod and then cried, 'Look!' and pointed as the shaving mirror beneath the flickering light fogged up with an invisible breath that spread out like a mushroom cloud. The toothpaste mug on the shelf below began to rock back and forth and then, with a squeaking sound, a clear spot appeared on the mist, like a full stop.

Abe was frowning. 'What is that?'

'Come on, Nedly!' Lil hissed under her breath. She could see him desperately trying to focus his energy on one trembling fingertip.

Abe stood up and moved towards the mirror. The dot grew a thin and shaky tail. It looked like a balloon on a string. 'What does that mean?' He peered at it, confused. Nedly slunk back.

'Is that it?' Lil mouthed at Nedly.

'It's hard to do it under pressure,' he moaned. 'I'm not used to having an audience.'

'Isn't that the whole point?' She rolled her eyes. 'Great!' Folding her arms and sitting back in the deck-chair she added, 'You've blown it.'

Abe looked at her quizzically. 'Are you talking to me?'

Nedly glowered at Lil. He gritted his teeth and strode back up to the mirror and then raised his finger up to the glass.

Abe seemed to sense his presence and stepped away. From where she was sitting Lil could see the hairs on the back of his neck rise. There was a squeak on the glass and the dot spread, becoming a hyphen. Lil sat forward urging Nedly on with her eyes. Abe pushed a shaking finger round his shirt collar.

The hyphen gained two vertical lines and became an 'H'.

A minute later a second line appeared beside it and then Nedly collapsed, exhausted.

'Hi?' Abe said. 'Hi?'

'He's saying "hi",' Lil explained.

'Thank you, Einstein,' Abe growled. 'I can

read it. I'm just trying to work out how you did it.'

'Grrrr!' Lil clenched her fists, exasperated. 'What more proof do you need?'

Abe coughed and adjusted his tie. When he finally spoke his voice was husky.

'You maybe think because I'm getting on a bit, and maybe I like the sauce too much, you can have a laugh on me.'

'I'm not laughing, Abe.'

'Well, neither am I.' Abe swiped his mug from the table and drank a large gulp. Then he sat back in the deck-chair, which collapsed, spilling the last of the tea down his shirt. He swore as he tried mopping it up with his tie. Then he sighed and lay back on the floor.

Lil tried out some sympathy. 'Look, I know it's a lot to take in but we think . . .'

'You and this ghost?' Abe didn't get up; he just lay there defeated, staring at the ceiling.

'Me and the ghost of Ned Stubbs. Nedly,' she corrected. 'We think it makes perfect sense. That's why the police didn't find any forensic evidence, why there were no witnesses – because the Firebug is a ghost!'

'Really.' Abe tipped back his hat with one finger.

Lil gaped at him. 'You don't believe me?'

'Would *you* believe you?' He clambered to his feet and kicked the unreliable deck-chair out of the way. 'You may have got me spooked in the beginning, but I'm all over that now.'

'You think I'm lying?' Lil glared at him, her lips puckered in a scowl. 'Well, isn't that nice? It so happened that a ghost saved your life yesterday, or did you think you got out of there all by yourself?' She spat the words out in Mandrel's face, pointing an accusatory finger for emphasis. 'You were out for the count, remember?' She shook her head scornfully.

Abe flinched back with a bruised look, but Lil was too furious to stop.

'You know what – I think we've spent just about enough time on you. I'm going to walk out of here in a minute and solve the Ned Stubbs case with or without you, but before I do you should know who's after you, because it might just save your life.' She paused and sucked in a breath. 'The ghost we saw just before the fire, the one who is trying to kill you, he had blonde hair and a large scar that runs down from his mouth and covers his neck.'

The detective snorted in disbelief. He started shaking his head but then something occurred to him and he narrowed his eyes sceptically.

Lil widened hers. 'You know who it is!'

'You've just described Leonard Owl.'

'Never heard of him.' She looked over at Nedly who shrugged back in the negative.

'Then you've probably seen a picture somewhere. He was before your time. Owl died in the fire at Rorschach, more than ten years ago, and no one has heard a peep from him since. I doubt that he has suddenly decided to rise up from the grave to go on a killing spree, but if –' he over-emphasised the word – '*if* he had, why would I be on his list?'

'You tell me.'

'You know so much all of sudden, why don't you tell me?'

Lil shrugged. 'Did you arrest him?'

Abe shook his head. 'He handed himself in. He wasn't much older than you when he confessed to burning the family estate to the ground. That's how he got that terrible scar: he went back in to save his pet goldfish from the flames. I mean, sure, he was dangerous and unbalanced, but the fire was a compulsion – he never meant to hurt anyone.'

'Maybe he's changed?' Lil suggested. 'It's worth checking out, though, isn't it? It makes sense that Owl is the perpetrator; a ghost can come and go almost without a trace, walk through locked doors, be invisible on CCTV. And now you tell us Owl's M.O. was arson! I'll bet it's his ghost that haunts the old asylum. It all fits, doesn't it?'

'All except for the bit about the spooks being real,' said Abe. 'That one's pretty hard to swallow.'

'Yesterday we – Nedly and I – did a bit of

271

poking around on our own. One of the orphans, Clark 'Babyface' Kennedy confessed that the night Nedly disappeared he was heading for the old asylum at Rorschach too. That's the best clue we've had so far. So even if you don't believe my theory about Owl you have to go there and follow up the lead on Ned Stubbs, don't you?'

'I think I'll sit this one out.'

Lil's eyes glistened fiercely. 'Fine. I can go by myself. I've got along perfectly well without you until now.' She gritted her teeth. 'But a boy died in this crummy town and people seem to think that doesn't matter. I thought we were about finding out who was responsible, and justice and all that stuff – and, if nothing else, someone actually paid you to find out, so shame on you if you don't see it through. At least you owe it to him to try. You owe it to me!'

Abe pursed his lips like he was about to play the trombone and his face took on a purplish tint in the blue-green light.

Lil persevered. 'Well, don't you?'

'Have you finished?' he growled.

Lil fixed him with a glare and folded her arms. 'You tell me.'

'OK,' he sighed. 'We'll go.' Lil grabbed her mac and headed for the door. Abe watched her in disbelief. 'Now?'

She shrugged in a way that meant, *obviously, why not?*

He gave her a bewildered look. 'Because it's getting dark . . . and they say the old asylum is haunted.'

'Right now the Ocean View Room is haunted, and anyway –' she raised one eyebrow at him – 'you don't believe in ghosts. Come on, we'll take a torch.'

Lil and Nedly waited near the basement steps while Abe went round to get the Zodiac. Nedly was going through the motions of scuffing his trainers against the kerb with a gloomy look on his face.

'Don't sweat it, Nedly,' Lil said. 'He'll come round.'

A cleaning firm was clearing up all the burnt

273

rubbish from Abe's old rooms. A scaffolding platform stacked with charred furniture and boxes was being lowered from the seventh floor.

'It's not that,' Nedly replied distractedly, watching the wisps of black paper floating down through the rain like birds, disintegrating into powder before they hit the ground. 'It just doesn't make sense. I've seen Owl before, I know I have, but when I saw him, I'm sure that he was alive.'

'But that doesn't make sense – you would only have been a baby when he died.'

'I told you it doesn't make sense.'

He kicked pointlessly at a piece of paper that had fallen into the gutter, barely rippling the water that swam over it. It was a photograph with curled and blackened edges. Ramon LeTeef's face was all but burnt away, only his small weak eyes and the mouth crammed full of sharp teeth remained.

At the newsstand on the corner was the latest edition of the *Herald*. The front cover showed a picture of Mayor Dean in a new, unsinged sheepskin coat, shaking the hands of a shady-looking business man as a new casino opened its doors to the public. There was no mention on the front cover about the arson spree or the Firebug Killer – as far as the *Herald* was concerned, he didn't exist at all.

Chapter 20

All Roads Lead to Rorschach

The Zodiac tore out of the city on a winding road that led into the hinterlands of Peligan. Overhead the wires crackled with the electricity from the pylons that strode across the landscape, bridging the gap between the city and the power station. Through the thick and muggy air a cool wind had started to blow; a storm was on its way.

They left the lights on and the engine running while Abe cut the rusty chain with his bolt-cutter attachment and pushed the old gates open. As they drove under the curved metal sign for Rorschach Asylum the car headlights picked up the road ahead, lighting the bony fingers of the trees that bent over the track like witches, and sweeping past the bedraggled lawns and thorn bushes, until they came to a gravelly halt in front of the building. The burnt-brick shell of the asylum loomed against the sky, as dark and empty as a black hole. An inauspicious bank of cloud moved over it like a ghostly road to somewhere.

Lil gasped as suddenly lightning rent the sky and the whole place lit up before them like a giant cackling face.

'I've never seen so many rabbits,' said Nedly.

Lil pulled her gaze from the horror that lay before them. 'Where?' She looked doubtfully at a thicket of grass. In the dark she couldn't see further than a few feet.

'Everywhere,' Nedly murmured.

'Damn this storm,' muttered Abe. 'Are you sure about this, kid? It's not too late to go back.'

Lil hoped that she didn't look as queasy as she felt and replied, 'I'm sure,' in a voice that sounded like she really wasn't.

As they climbed the stone steps to the front door, Abe traced the inscription above it with his torch. '*Pulvio et Umbra Sumus*,' he said. 'We are Dust and Shadow.' Thunder rolled in the distance.

Nedly was trembling, barely visible in the dim moonlight. 'I've got a bad feeling about this,' he said.

'About what?' Lil tried to keep her voice level.

'Everything,' he said ominously.

Lil felt her fingertips tingle and go numb as she pushed at the door; it creaked open like a yawn to reveal a dank entrance hall. Grey water pooled on the green and white tiles, black powdery smudges streaked the walls and a sweeping staircase led up to the first floor. As they moved further in they were accosted by a powerful smell of mouldering damp.

'*Upstairs*,' whispered Nedly.

Lil pointed the way to Abe without speaking

and they gingerly climbed the stairs. The banister was tar-coloured and just as sticky. Wafer-thin scraps of soot peeled off the walls as they passed and floated down. The torch beam swung round and dropped suddenly as Abe put his foot through the rotten wood of the last stair and fell over with a gasp. He hauled himself to his feet, shaking, and brushed the brick dust and splinters off his trousers. Then he gave himself a quick slap on the cheek to snap his wits back into gear.

Lil picked up the torch from where it had rolled on the landing and pointed it up ahead in time to see Nedly turn right and begin walking. A blank expression had fallen over his face; he moved automatically, retracing his own tracks as if he didn't have a choice.

Long corridors and lonely footsteps. The asylum didn't feel empty. Lil could hear the rain dripping and pooling on the floors through the gaps in the burnt rafters. They passed room after room. Where the doors were open they could see that ivy had crept in and loosened bricks, and thin iron bedsteads with broken springs were stacked up against the walls. Abandoned tables and chairs had been knocked over and left; hospital gurneys were marooned in treatment rooms.

'We don't want to get lost in here,' Abe warned. 'This place is like a labyrinth.'

They moved quickly through the corridors, trying to breathe quietly – every footstep felt like they were making too much noise. Abe's heavy feet ground shattered glass, trailing Lil's torch beam as it jumped along the floor.

At the edge of the east wing, where the fire had started, only the building's skeleton remained: the brick chimney stacks, the walls, and the roof, which looked like it had been staved in, leaving a few black rafters poking out like old bones. A large milk-coloured bird flew out from the wreckage and fluttered towards the sky.

Abe skidded on one of the melted vinyl floor tiles, which were blistered and slippery with rainwater. He clutched a blackened fire extinguisher to keep his balance and nearly knocked it off the wall. 'A lot of good that was,' he grumbled. 'Hasn't even been used.'

The blaze hadn't reached the furthest rooms of the east wing; as they crept along the corridor, passing the moonlit windows, Lil peered into the soft, sinister darkness of isolation cells that were lined in padded tiles, a stark 'Wash Room', which contained nothing but a large metal bath tub, and the day room with its charred easy chairs and gloomy walls.

She was just in time to see Nedly disappear round a corner. She hissed at him to 'Wait,' but by the time she reached the end of the corridor he had vanished. She heard Abe huffing and puffing not too far behind so she supposed it was safe to gather speed and catch up with Nedly, following the stream of cold air that pursued him.

But Nedly was nowhere to be seen. She turned back and found herself in a long corridor studded with windows. Grey moonlight glimmered through the film of murk on the glass. Lil walked a few steps and her torchlight flickered. She stopped. A cold breath of a breeze blew past and the tattered curtains fluttered like moth wings.

She realised that the sound of footsteps behind her had faded away. 'Abe?' she called out.

There was no answer. Somehow she was all alone.

She was midway down the corridor when her torch went out. Lil took a deep, steadying breath and then banged the torch against her palm. It buzzed dimly and then with a ping it failed entirely. She let her eyes adjust to the pixelated darkness and set off again. She was sure that the corridor branched off to the right up ahead and so she headed for it.

As she walked purposefully onwards, counting her steps under her breath, Lil felt someone approaching behind her and turned, but there was no one. A movement at the end of the corridor caught her eye, as a dark shape slipped out of view.

Lil's stomach jumped. She turned back, sweating now, walking faster towards the exit. In the fuzz she saw darkness amassing in the doorway; it formed a shadow that fell across the hall.

'Abe?' she whispered not loud enough for anyone to hear.

Maybe she should retrace her steps again? Go back and find Abe or go forward and find Nedly? She looked back the way she had come, and as she turned something moved, a reflection in one of the darkened windows. She heard a door shut somewhere.

OK, Lil thought. *Deep breaths.*

It was the place. It was spooky; there were rumours that it was haunted. Well, Lil didn't scare easily and she didn't believe in ghosts. No, wait, she did. But ghosts can't hurt you.

But they can, she thought. She walked on, each footstep falling quietly, swiftly. She thought she heard a voice, someone calling her name. She called out more loudly: 'Abe? I'm here!'

The footsteps grew louder. If someone was

there, they were close. Lil turned sharply, but all she could see was darkness moving down the corridor like a wave and a terrible feeling that something was hidden within it.

'Abe?'

As Lil spun to face the figure that loomed up in front of her the breath left her lungs in a hurry and turned into a loud and blood-curdling scream.

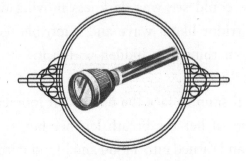

Chapter 21

The Chief Consultant's Office

'Are you trying to give me a heart attack?' Abe collapsed against the wall, grey-faced in the weak moonlight and panting. He cast Lil a grim look.

'I was scared! *You* scared *me*,' hissed Lil, jabbing an accusing finger at him.

'I scared you! What were you doing hiding here in the shadows?' He punched himself in the chest. 'I'm lucky the old ticker didn't stop right there.'

'I wasn't hiding, I was just standing still, wondering where everyone was, because you didn't answer,' Lil fired back. 'I was calling for you.'

'Because, Wing Nut, I thought we were supposed to be sneaking around so I was trying to keep what we in the business call a "low profile"!' He shook his head. 'That's the last time I let you carry the torch; you left me for dust back there.'

'Take it,' said Lil, shoving it into his hands. 'It doesn't work anyway.'

Abe twisted the end and the bulb flickered back to life.

Lil scowled. 'Well, it didn't work before.'

A quiet voice interrupted them. Nedly was standing at the end of the corridor. In the darkness he seemed to emit a pearly glow and his large eyes looked like hollows. Lil ran up to where he had been standing just in time to see him melt through a heavy wooden door.

She wiped the soot off the plaque and then

snatched the torch out of Abe's hand and shone it on the inscription.

'"Dr Hans Carvel – Chief Consultant". Abe! Look at this. The murdered prison doctor, Carvel, worked here at Rorschach! That's how Owl knew him.' She tried the door but it was locked fast. 'Can we get in?'

Abe pulled out his skeleton key attachment and after a few moments of fiddling with the lock he gave up and shoved the door open with a shoulder barge.

It was like a room that had been asleep for a hundred years, and was coated with thick dust and strung with spider webs. Lil choked on the pungent mustiness. The thick door had protected the room from the worst of the fire and any draughts of fresh air that might have entered it. A green mummified apple sat on the furry grey surface of a once-polished desk. Lil gave it a poke and it disintegrated into powder.

She turned to a series of grey-metal filing cabinets leaning against one wall. The labels on the drawers indicated that they contained records for the patients and the staff that lived and worked at Rorschach. She stepped back while Abe jemmied the lock open with one of the pincers of his driving attachment and then held out his hand to get the torch back.

Lil pretended she hadn't seen the gesture and tightened her grip. Angling the beam into the cabinet she rummaged in the staff files following her hunch.

'Carvel worked here; maybe some of the others did too. Kreutz trained as a nurse. I'll bet she's in here.' She pulled out a file. 'There! So that just leaves you, the mayor and McConkey without a connection to the asylum.' Lil flicked through the alphabetised files until she reached 'M' and pulled out the file triumphantly and began scanning it.

'I'll bet McConkey was a security guard here too, before the fire,' Abe said quickly, before Lil had a chance to.

'Wrong!' said Lil. 'He was an orderly.' Abe ground his teeth and held up his hands as if to say *what's the difference?* But Lil was on a roll.

'So it looks like all three people who were killed last week were survivors of the original fire. So . . .' She gesticulated frantically. 'Maybe Owl was finishing the job he started when he torched the asylum all those years ago!'

Abe brought her back down to earth. 'Nice theory, but where do I fit in?' he said flatly. 'I've never had anything much to do with the asylum or Leonard Owl. Anyway, as I recall, four members of staff survived the original fire, so how come he stopped at three?'

'What makes you think he's stopped . . .' said Lil darkly. 'Maybe they're next on the list?'

'Maybe it's not Leonard Owl at all . . . maybe those fires were accidents and the victims having worked at Rorschach is a coincidence.'

'You don't believe that.'

Abe shrugged. 'At the moment all we're doing is hypothesising about the existence of spirits and poking around in an old building. I'm not sure what I believe any more.'

Lil pulled out Leonard Owl's file. It was yellowed and mouldy with age. At the beginning was an admittance form, and attached to that was a photograph. She held it out to Nedly.

'This was the one you saw, right? It's Leonard Owl.'

Nedly craned his neck round, trying to get a look at it.

'Sorry,' said Lil. 'I forgot.'

She turned the picture round again and held it up.

Owl's hair was silver-blonde, his face pale except for the shiny pink scar tissue on his chin and neck, which made his jaw look separate from the rest of his face like a ventriloquist's dummy. He looked no more than fifteen years old and his grey eyes were melancholy and apologetic.

'That's him, but he's older now.'

'Nedly has given us a positive I.D. on Owl,' Lil told Abe.

'Right.' The detective looked ominously around trying to pinpoint the alleged ghost's position in the room.

'He's right behind you.'

Abe jumped. He shot a furious glance over

his shoulder as the hair on the back of his neck pricked up. He wiped the cold sweat from his forehead with the back of his sleeve.

'Don't be angry with him. He's not trying to scare you.'

'Who said anyone is scared?'

'He can't help giving people the creeps. It's part of his – condition.'

'Him being dead, is that what you mean?' The torch bulb flickered and the air turned a few degrees colder.

'It's not a nice feeling,' Lil said in a quiet voice, 'when people don't believe in you.'

Abe nodded to himself. 'Don't I know it.' He sighed. 'Look, let me get this straight. You're saying that Leonard Owl, a ghost, has been starting fires and burning people to death all over the city. And you think that when Ned Stubbs, or Nedly, stumbled across him hiding out in this asylum, he killed him too?'

'Correct!' said Lil, thinking: *At last!*

'So, what are we going to do about it?'

'We stop him. We bring him in!'

Abe gave her a long, hard stare filled with meaning. Lil frowned back at him and then released her eyebrows. They rose sky-high as the gravity of the situation finally dawned on her. 'We can't stop him,' she said in a small voice. 'We don't know how.'

'Correct.'

'There must be a way.' She looked helplessly at Nedly but he wasn't listening. Lil dropped her voice to a whisper. 'There must be. He killed Nedly.'

'No,' said Nedly. 'He didn't.' He was staring at one of the pictures that was hanging on the wall. Grey splotches of damp had sprouted in the corners of the frame and the glass was smudged and dusty. It was a group photograph of the staff sitting in rigid formation on the lawn area in front of the asylum. The lawn was clipped short and smooth like a bowling green and rambling roses grew on either side of the steps. All the staff were wearing white uniforms.

Lil moved closer to him.

Nedly's face had grown pale, his skin so thin he was almost translucent.

'He did it. That's the man who murdered me.'

Nedly pointed at the photograph, past the neat line-up of doctors. Lil wiped away the dust and then shone the torch at the smeared glass. There, standing on the steps behind the staff, was another man. He was not part of the official group but he was looking into the camera anyway. 'Him.'

He was pointing at a man with deep-set colourless eyes and a hairless brow, a man wearing the blue tunic of an inmate. His hands were held patiently together, and there was a thin covering of wispy hair on his head.

There was something familiar about him; Lil had seen his picture before: on a mug shot in Abe's Lucan Road Mob file, and on the back of a book. His face might also have been stuck on the map at the Mingo, but the thick black cross marking him out as 'deceased' would have disguised him. 'Cornelius Gallows!' she exclaimed. 'Abe, Nedly says that he's the man who killed him!'

Abe shook his head at the photograph.

'Gallows is long dead.' His gaze pointlessly searched the empty space by the wall. 'He died in the fire along with Leonard Owl and more than twenty other inmates.'

'Gallows was alive when I saw him just a year ago,' Nedly insisted. 'He was alive when he killed me, and so was Owl. He can't have died in that fire.'

'Did they ever find Gallows' body?' Lil asked Abe.

'He was burnt to a crisp. Maybe beyond recognition,' he admitted.

Lil yanked open the drawer of patient files A–G and flicked through from the back. She pulled out a thick cardboard wallet and thumbed through the papers inside.

'Here,' she said eventually. 'This is the last dated report in the file.'

PSYCHIATRIC REPORT BY
DR HANS CARVEL, RORSCHACH
ASYLUM, PELIGAN CITY
on the case of CORNELIUS GALLOWS

The patient has been diagnosed as a psychopath with extreme narcissistic tendencies. Cornelius is generally quiet and distant but has been subject to sudden rages. In group sessions he has voiced paranoid delusions about myself and Dr Lankin stealing his research ideas. Undoubtedly he has a brilliant mind but absolutely no morals, no ethics, no compassion.

His record shows few disturbances since his committal and no disciplinary procedures have been initiated. However, Dr Lankin has asked me to record that Cornelius is beginning to exhibit a concerning degree of influence over a fellow patient, Leonard Owl. Leonard is impressionable and eager to please and has been regularly observed to be watching Cornelius attentively as if seeking approval.

'You know what I think?' said Lil. 'I think they were in league together. Maybe the reason we can't find a link is that you weren't on Owl's list, you were on Gallows', along with the rest of the Lucan Road Mob. They betrayed him, you put him away and Carvel kept him locked up.'

Abe nodded.

'So maybe Owl is doing this out of loyalty. Or because he thinks that's what Gallows would have wanted.'

Abe rubbed at the stubble on his chin. 'I could buy that. He was a fairly messed-up boy; I don't expect being a ghost has made him any saner.'

'Now, where exactly do you fit into all this?' Lil pondered, looking at Nedly.

'Come on,' he said miserably. 'There's a room we haven't been to yet.'

Lil and Abe followed the ghost of Ned Stubbs as he walked slowly down the corridor, as if he was re-enacting his part in a macabre play. When he reached the door that said 'Treatment Room' he put out his hand and it swung open before him.

In the centre of the room was an upright wooden contraption that looked like an electric chair, with a beaten metal head-cap and wires along the arm rests. Sitting on the chair was a horrible woollen toy.

'Wool!' breathed Lil.

'It was here,' said Nedly. 'This is where I died.'

They entered the room in silence. The atmosphere was oppressively sad. Lil walked over to the chair and picked up the toy that rested there.

'That's what I was looking for,' murmured Nedly.

'Did you find him?' asked Lil.

Nedly nodded slowly.

Wool, Babyface's knitted humpty, was the most sinister toy Lil had ever seen. It had no mouth or nose, only round, staring white felt eyes, one of which had become partly unstuck and hung down like a wink. A tuft of black woollen hair sprouted from the apex of its head. It had thin knitted arms and legs, which were joined to the egg-shaped body like chipolatas on strings. At the end of each limb someone had sewn a little silver bell.

Lil picked it up by one leg, using the tip of her finger and thumb, and held it at arm's length to examine it with her torch. Wool twirled like an aerial acrobat, a topsy-turvy pirouette, and as it spun the little bells tinkled. The sound travelled away from them to a very dark place in between the eaves and the scorched rafters.

Then they heard it. A small voice, muffled at first but growing louder. Someone was crying; it was a whimpering, sobbing noise that filled the empty corridors.

'No!' Nedly gasped in a voice too quiet for anyone to hear.

Lil snapped her head round to look at him. 'Nedly?'

He was staring at the door with a look of pure dread. 'Someone's coming,' he said.

'We shouldn't have come here . . .' began Lil.

'It's too late,' whispered Nedly.

Then the sound of crying stopped and the laughing began.

Chapter 22

'Men Have Called Me Mad'

Cornelius Gallows stepped into the doorway carrying an old brown metal oil lamp in one hand and a revolver in the other. His face carried more lines than his mug shot and his eyes had sunken even further back in their sockets. He was wearing a dirty lab coat and a black rubber gas mask worn high over his head like an insect-faced hat; around it his fine hair was standing on end as though someone had rubbed a balloon over it.

'Detective Mandrel, we meet again!'

Abe narrowed his eyes. 'Cornelius Gallows. So you're not dead after all.'

'No, I'm very much alive, as you can see. While the fire raged in the east wing, I calmly strolled into one of the consultant's offices and took his I.D. and certification; I merely ensured that the doctor in question was in the path of the blaze and was, therefore, incinerated beyond recognition. Then I just had to put on this precious lab coat and walk right out of here. The emergency services actually helped me to safety; they assumed that I was one of the doctors!' Gallows laughed, the lantern up-lighting his face to ghoulish effect.

'But you're not a doctor, are you, Cornelius – you're a patient.'

'How dare you!' Two pinpricks of blush appeared on Gallows' sallow cheeks.

'You were struck off years ago, when you published that wacko book.' Abe sidled towards him. 'And I should have known you'd be here – in the madhouse where you belong.'

Gallows pointed the revolver at him threateningly. 'It suits me perfectly: no disturbance – until now of course – just peace and quiet for my work. It even has its own graveyard.' He gave a withering laugh. 'I know you're trying to goad me, detective, trying to make me lose my temper like the judge did at the trial. You won't catch me out this time. Not that it matters; as far as anyone knows, I'm dead, so you can't convict me. Officially I don't exist.'

'We know you're not dead. We'll tell on you,' said Lil.

Gallows shifted his gaze to Lil. 'Ah, you're assuming that you will be getting out of here alive. On the contrary, little girl – you will both be quite dead by morning.'

'No!' said Lil.

'Yes!' said Gallows, his pale eyes burning with a cold flame. 'Everyone who gets in my way comes to a sticky end, mark my words. No one even noticed when I was bumping off those small-time hoodlums, my former henchmen who sang like canaries at the trial. No one batted an eye – except that interfering news pamphlet and you, Mandrel, always poking that sticky beak of yours where it doesn't belong.' He spat out the words. 'You blundering oaf. Even when you finally managed to capture Ramon, who isn't even particularly smart, the turncoat split on me and got away scot-free. But I'll make him pay.

'You all deserve to die. I've been patient, oh yes! Revenge is indeed a dish best served cold. For nine years I worked here in the darkness, until my experimental procedure was complete, until I, Dr C. Gallows PhD, finally held the secret of life after death. Until I was ready to create the ultimate criminal.'

'That explains all the rabbits. Gallows must have been experimenting on them all this time,' Lil mumured under her breath. 'They were ghosts too – that's why I couldn't see them.' She looked at Nedly but he had retreated into a corner, as far away from Gallows as he could get.

Gallows' flimsy hair swayed in the unnatural draughts that swirled around him, the whites of his eyes shone in the gloom and his lips trembled excitedly.

'One year ago, with my research complete, I put my theory into practice: I weaponised Leonard Owl.'

'You killed him, you mean,' said Lil.

'I turned him into an instrument of fear.' Gallows waved the gun at her dismissively. Every day for the last year we have practised until sad little Leonard Owl was ready to become Mr Glimmer: a disembodied spirit that cannot be seen, stopped or caught. I made him who he is today.'

'You murdered him.'

'Owl knew what he was doing. He sacrificed himself in the name of science.'

'He just wanted Gallows to like him,' said Nedly miserably. He wasn't looking at the evil genius any more but a point near the window where a cobweb of ice crystals was forming on the glass.

304

Out of the corner of her eye Lil saw Abe's torchlight flicker and wondered if Owl was there too, listening in.

'You're just using him,' she said to Gallows.

'Of course I am. Why else would I have spent ten years of my life with a quivering idiot who can't stop lighting matches?'

'He thought he was your friend.'

'I don't need friends. Leonard is useful to me. Well, he was. Now, I've realised that if you want to scare someone to death, you have to find someone really scary. Leonard's just a troubled boy; he never really enjoyed frightening people. But I've got a new line coming out – I've found myself the perfect source to recruit my subjects from –' Gallows held a finger to his own mouth to stop the words – 'but that's a secret. I'm not going to fall for that old trick of revealing my master plan and then risk you escaping from the elaborate death I have planned for you to thwart me at the final hour.

'My reign of terror is almost ready to begin, but first I just have one last loose end to tie up

305

and it will give my new accomplice a chance to flex his muscles, so to speak. Mr Grip, I call him – he hasn't been out much so he's eager to get his hands dirty.' He laughed maniacally. 'Oh yes! I will give Peligan City the fright of its life!'

The flame of Gallows' gas lamp guttered.

'Mr Glimmer can still have his fun. Tonight there will be a second fire at Rorschach Asylum, and tomorrow the papers will report that a scruffy ex-police detective and a big-eared child perished in it . . . and no one will know why!'

There was no more time for subtlety. 'You don't have to do what he says,' Lil yelled at the window. 'Don't listen to him!'

'Ah, but he does,' said Gallows, picking up the knitted humpty and shaking it.

'It's Wool,' cried Nedly. 'It's controlling him.'

The little bells tinkled and a look of dread crossed Nedly's face.

'He has to do exactly what I say, when I say it. Leonard was smitten when he found that filthy toy.' He pointed at Wool. 'So I thought that as a special treat I'd bind his spirit to it. That's the key, you see. It's my remote control.'

Lil backed away from the window as Nedly stepped into what she calculated to be Owl's path, to shield herself and Abe. She could see his shoulders trembling in the moonlight.

'But why did you have to kill Nedly, I mean Ned Stubbs?' she asked Gallows.

'Who?'

'Ned Stubbs,' Lil repeated with dry contempt.

Gallows rubbed his hairless chin with mock thoughtfulness. 'Was he another orderly?'

'No!'

'A patient?'

'No, he was an eleven-year-old orphan!'

'Was that his name?' He gave Lil an icy stare. 'I'd quite forgotten about him. He got in the way. Tried to mess up my experiment with his last-minute heroics. If he hadn't been trying to free Owl, then he wouldn't have got electrocuted. The correct timing of the experiment was essential. In fact, he could have ruined everything.' Gallows eyed Lil scornfully.

'Children shouldn't poke around where they don't belong. There are very clear signs on the gate that say "No Entry" and "Trespassers will be Prosecuted" and "Danger".'

Lil's hands formed into fists. She could feel herself shaking with anger.

'It wasn't all fun and games for me either, little girl,' Gallows continued. 'I had to bury them both, digging the graves myself. Well, I dug a grave and put them both in it. It was abominably hard work, I can tell you.' He pondered. 'If I'd thought it through I would have got Leonard to dig it before I killed him. Oh well, hindsight's a wonderful thing.'

Gallows looked up with an expression of disgust. 'Is that you snivelling, Mr Glimmer? Stop it immediately; you're embarrassing us both,' he hissed in the general direction of the cold spot beside the window. 'If you can't act like a proper henchman, I'll have to dispose of you.' Gallows viciously kicked Wool across the floor with a sweep of his foot. Wool bounced off the skirting board, and then lay still, face down, one arm outstretched as if reaching for something.

Gallows cleared his throat and continued, 'Now, where was I? One final act and my revenge will be complete; Ramon LeTeef must pay for his betrayal, and he will. Once Mr Grip gets hold of him – he'll be begging me to kill him!'

Abe snorted. 'Good luck with finding him, Cornelius. LeTeef vanished straight after the trial and no one has set eyes on him since. Or didn't you know that?'

Gallows narrowed his eyes. 'Are you serious?'

'Deadly,' Abe replied.

Gallows sighed. 'No. I mean, are you seriously telling me that you don't know where he is?'

'No one does.'

Gallows allowed himself a self-satisfied smile. 'I do. I have always known. Surely it doesn't take a genius to work it out?' He looked at Lil; she stared blankly back at him. 'No? Oh, well, maybe it does.'

Abe was losing patience. He took a step

309

towards Gallows. 'Look, I have no problem with LeTeef getting iced. But why don't you just save yourself a lot of bother and tell me where he is, and I'll put him away for you.'

Lil was furious. 'Abe! Aren't you going to say, "You won't get away with it!"?'

Abe shrugged. 'If he can find Ramon LeTeef and make him pay, I'll be happy to see justice done at long last.'

'But he killed Nedly.'

Abe clenched his jaw. He nodded to himself, ashamed. 'You're right, kid. I'm sorry, I forgot. You won't get away with it!' he yelled at Gallows.

Gallows shook his head derisively.

Abe's eyes were on the revolver that was hanging heavy in Gallows' limp fingers. 'You're waving that gun around all right,' he said. 'But you don't have the first clue about how to use it.'

Gallows placed the gun in the large pocket of his lab coat. 'I won't need it.'

'Is that right? Ha! You haven't caught us yet,'

310

said Abe. 'And I won't go down without a fight.'

'Yes, detective, you will,' said Gallows, and he lowered his gas mask as the room filled up with a cloud of yellow mist.

Chapter 23

Death Trap

Blackness gave way to a blurry blue light and the room warped as it came into focus. The storm raged outside; rain was beating down on the crumbling walls of the asylum and the wind howled through the broken chimneys.

Lil shook her head to clear it and a dizzying headache awoke. Her arms and legs were numb, her shoulders were sore and her ears were filled with the sawing sound of heavy breathing. 'Abe!' she hissed. 'Abe, wake up!'

The breathing sound stopped, snorted and then continued.

'Nedly?' Lil whispered. 'Can you hear me?' Then louder, 'Nedly?' There was no answer. They were alone.

She and Abe were bound fast together, sitting back to back on old hospital chairs, their hands and feet tied with nylon rope.

'Abe!' Lil knocked the back of her head against his.

'What the . . . !' He awoke with a gasp and immediately began thrashing about trying to free himself.

'Abe! Stop wriggling. There's no point; the ropes are too tight.'

He went still. 'Where are we?'

Lil could just make out a blue square shape that looked like a window with bars.

'It's some kind of cell, I suppose. I think he released a sort of sleeping gas and then when we were out cold, he tied us up.' There was a sickly sweet smell on the air like medicated icing sugar. A flash of lightning bleached the room white and in that split second Lil saw something that turned her blood cold.

A cat's cradle of red string criss-crossed the room, from the floor to the ceiling. At the centre of it, the threads tied to his pink, thin arms, was Wool, with the tiny bells in its hands, its eyes white and empty. Lil and Abe were ensnared below, like a couple of flies in a spider's web.

'If we touch any one of those threads it will wake Wool up and he'll call to Owl.'

Abe gave a humph, the sort of sound that inferred, *now look at the mess you've got us into*.

'Don't blame me,' said Lil.

'Well, it wasn't my idea to come here.'

'No, but you didn't have to tag along,' Lil pointed out.

'You asked me to come!' he huffed. 'Anyway, this is *my* case, remember? If anyone is tagging along, it's you.'

'So, it's *your* case now – well, you wouldn't have got very far without me and Nedly.'

Abe took a deep breath. 'We're not getting anywhere sitting here and arguing about it.'

Lil pursed her lips, thought about not replying and then said, 'You're the one that's arguing.'

Abe sighed. 'Can you work the ropes loose on your side?'

Lil tried to move her wrists but only succeeded in rubbing some skin off. She tried to wiggle her shoulders back and forth but she was held fast.

'They're too tight.'

Abe spent a minute twisting his arms round, trying to loosen the ropes tying his wrists. There was a slap as something hit the ground.

Lil tried to look around. 'Abe?'

'I managed to get one hand free,' he said flatly.

Lightning flashed again and Lil saw Abe's prosthetic hand on the floor, palm upwards.

'Great,' she sighed.

'Hang about. I might be on to something.' Without his prosthetic hand the rope was looser. Abe worked it down over his wrist to freedom and then slipped the other hand out of the slack.

The next flash came with a ripple of thunder and Lil involuntarily glanced up. Wool was still hanging there with the same blank expression, staring emptily at her.

Abe reached for Lil's hands and began fumbling to untie the knots that bound them.

'Ouch! Ow! Stop!' said Lil. 'You're nipping me.'

'Sorry,' said Abe, not sounding that sorry, 'but we're in a kind of life-or-death situation and this is my driving attachment, not my unpicking-knots attachment.'

'You have an unpicking-knots attachment?'

'I adapted it from a crochet hook.'

Lil swore and gritted her teeth. 'Ow!' Tears came to her eyes.

'Almost got it – there!'

She wriggled her hands and the ropes loosened. Her fingers prickled uncomfortably as the feeling came back to them.

Abe chuckled triumphantly to himself. 'Right,

let's undo these cords that are tying us to the chair and then our feet and then . . . Cripes, this is tricky.'

He was trying to pinch the ones round himself with his pincers. Lil was plucking at hers with her fingertips – neither one of them were getting anywhere and they hadn't even started on the ones round their ankles.

'The angle's all wrong.' Abe cursed. 'OK, I've got another plan. We'll both lean to the left and topple the chairs. Once we're crumpled up against the floor we should get a bit of slack on the rope; if we can wriggle free, then I can get to my Swiss Army hand and extract the letter-opening attachment. I can saw through the ties round our ankles and then we just have to negotiate our way through the tangle of threads without waking that egg thing, and get to the door.'

'What do we do when we reach the door?'

'We'll worry about that when we get there. Now, ready? On three. One, two, three!'

The chair stayed firm.

'What's wrong with this thing? Is it bolted to the ground? Give it another go,' he growled. 'On three – and this time really swing out to the left. OK?'

The chair wobbled. Abe sat up straight. He snorted.

'I meant my left – we both lean to my left.'

'Well, it's my right.'

'Thank you for pointing that out. Now – let's both lean – towards the door.'

'OK.'

'On three.'

The chair fell straight away and landed with a smack on the floor.

The linoleum was coated in a sticky dust and smelt of old wax polish and disinfectant. Lil tried to raise her head but gave up and let her forehead collect a grey rim of dust as she inched her way out of the ropes that bound them. Once she was free, Abe was able to slip the ropes off his shoulders and reach for the letter opener. He located the torch from his mac pocket and grudgingly handed it to Lil. It took him several minutes to cut the last of the ties with the slender knife, until finally they were free.

Slowly getting to their feet, they rubbed the life back into their legs and then nervously moved forward. Lil shone the torchlight back and forth to pick out the string that ensnared them, but it became harder to navigate safe passage as they neared the wall, where the threads hung low and were nailed into the floor like guy ropes.

Using a mixture of crouching, jumping and limbo techniques they had almost made it when a single thread caught and knocked Abe's hat to the floor. It wasn't a hard tug, but it was enough. The sound of the tiny bell cut through the air like a fairy death knell, a soft *tinkle tinkle*. They both froze as they heard it.

'Almost made it,' muttered Abe, retrieving his hat and frowning angrily at it.

'It's too late to worry,' Lil told him with more confidence than she felt. 'Let's just go for it. We have to get out of here, and fast.'

Lightning flashed, temporarily blinding them, and a second later thunder split the air. The storm was overhead now and the temperature in the room had already started falling.

'He's coming,' whispered Lil, trying to keep the panic out of her voice as part of the web where the hat had caught came loose and drooped over Abe, looping over his neck and shoulders. She tried to free him but her hands were clammy and her fingers couldn't get a grip without pulling hard and disturbing Wool again. The air was full of whispers and she could feel the hairs on the back of her neck rising.

They heard a creak and then doors started banging along the corridor, juddering open and closed with unnatural speed.

'Leave it!' shouted Lil over the noise. 'We've got nothing to lose. Just drag it!'

The banging stopped. The torch flickered out.

They froze in the total darkness.

'Don't move,' whispered Abe.

A floorboard creaked.

'It's two against one,' said Abe. 'We can take him between us.'

And do what with him, Lil thought and she shivered as an icy breath whispered across her cheek and her stomach somersaulted.

They stood motionless, barely breathing. A peel of high-pitched laughter rang out; it seemed to come from all around them. The little bells began tinkling frantically, as if someone had plucked all the threads at once. Thunder crashed, lightning blinked on and off, and through the glaring strobe effect Lil could see Wool staring impassively back at them, its pink chipolata arms waving.

'Go!' cried Abe. 'Now!' And they scrambled to the door. The broken threads fell around them, snagging on their legs. Wool was pulled to the floor and dragged behind them, tinkling.

Abe finally kicked himself free, grabbed the door handle and began furiously pulling at it.

'It's no good – we're trapped. It's locked from the outside.'

'Nedly!' Lil murmured to herself. 'Where are you?'

Ice crystals were spreading across the glass. It was freezing but beads of sweat were still glistening on Abe's brow.

'Grrr-aah!' Abe bellowed as the door knob came off in his hand.

Chapter 24

The Revenge of Leonard Owl

'Just keep calm,' shouted Abe, alternately hammering his fist and pincer on the door. After a few useless kicks and a number of interesting swear words he put his shoulder to the wood and started furiously ramming it.

Lil pounded the torch against her palm a few times until it sprang back to life, and then she whisked it this way and that. Shapes moved out of the corner of her eye and she tried to follow them with the beam of light, while shadows jumped across the walls. Then the lightning struck again and in the blinding dark that followed it Lil couldn't see anything at all; there was only maniacal, shrieking laughter, which drowned out all other sounds and rent the air like rusty knives.

'Abe,' she whispered.

Abe was occupied with trying to jemmy the door frame with his pincers.

'Abe!'

'Will somebody stop that damned laughing?' Abe bellowed. 'It's driving me crazy!'

'Stop!' Lil cried out. She ran over to Wool, picking it up by its hair. 'Stop!' she shouted, throwing it to the floor and stamping on it.

But the laughter just grew louder. Lil kicked the doll across the room in frustration. Its bells tinkled mischievously.

There was a click and a noise like scraping metal. The door opened out suddenly and Abe fell through, landing on the floor.

Lil gasped, ran into the corridor and helped him to his feet.

'Nedly!' Lil spun round searching the space with the torchlight but Nedly was nowhere to be seen. 'Where are you?'

Abe looked suspiciously at the padlock and chain, now hanging free. 'What do you call that?' he said, peering at the lock.

'A lucky break,' said Lil. 'Gallows didn't know about our secret weapon; he couldn't see Nedly. He must have worked out how to unpick the lock,' she said admiringly. 'Now, where is he?' She shouted, 'Nedly?' and then much louder, 'NEDLY!'

Abe looked at the lock for a second more and frowned. 'What if it wasn't Nedly? It could be a trap.'

Lil sniffed the air. 'You smell that? It's smoke. Come on!' She tried the doors on either side as they went. 'Which way should we go? Nedly?'

'Where is he?' Abe snapped.

Lil shone her torch left and right. It all looked the same. Her heartbeat quickened, a draught tickled her spine. 'Owl's coming – quick!'

Further down the hallway a door flapped suddenly open. They limped towards it uncertainly. It was a stairwell.

'Down here!' she called out.

They half ran, half tripped down the stairs and burst out of the doors at the other end.

'This way!' yelled Lil, running hell for leather down another identical-looking corridor – then she skidded suddenly to a halt.

Her torch beam glanced off the smoke that was billowing up from under the door at the far end; orange lights danced behind the reinforced glass. It was getting hot, flames were licking at the frame, and then the door blew open and the fire leapt to the ceiling.

'Fire!' shouted Abe. 'Back the other way!'

'What other way?'

'Any other way, just run!'

The laughter cackled and rang out in the corridors. It echoed off the walls.

To their left a door banged open and shut. They both turned to watch it.

'It's not Nedly,' said Lil. 'I can't see him.'

327

The door swung slowly open again and this time it stayed open.

'Maybe it's a trap?'

'Maybe it's a lift shaft?'

'Maybe it's a way out?'

It was. The door led onto a rickety cast-iron fire escape that zigzagged down to the ground. Lil led the way. The staircase groaned and swayed as the rivets holding it to the wall loosened from the crumbling brick. They held their arms over their heads and flinched from showers of broken glass, which fell past them every time a window exploded. Abe had to jump the last few steps before the staircase swung free and collapsed on the lawn.

When they had reached a safe distance from the asylum inferno, Lil and Abe lay on the boggy grass, for once thankful for the rain pelting down on them. Rorschach was lit up like a bonfire; its huge shadow jumped across the lawn, and black rafters dropped into the flames like matchsticks.

Lil looked up into one of the windows and thought she could just make out a limpid figure amongst the flames, a shadow against the light. He was holding an egg-shaped toy. Then the window shattered, flames burst from the frame and the figure was gone.

'Do you think that's the end of Leonard Owl?' she asked Abe.

'That weird woollen egg thing won't survive those temperatures.' Abe pondered. 'I suppose if he's bound to it then maybe once it's destroyed he'll have to move on, or whatever they do.'

'I hope so,' said Lil. She looked past the scorched lawn and into the dark woodland that surrounded them. 'Still no sign of Nedly.' She tried to keep her voice from quavering. 'You don't think he's gone too?'

Abe frowned uncomfortably. 'Who knows? We better get out of here, kiddo. You can be sure that this fire will be seen for miles around and I don't want to be here to answer any awkward questions when the emergency services arrive.'

They shook the rain off their coats and jumped into the car. Lil bundled into the passenger seat as Abe flipped down the sunshield, caught the key in the pincers of his driving attachment and shoved it in the ignition. The car made a strained choking sound. He turned it again.

'Come on, come on!' Lil urged.

Abe shot her a look that said, *I'm going as fast as I can; it's not my fault the car won't start and I would probably be able to think more clearly about the best way to get the motor running if I didn't have you yelling 'Come on!' in my earhole every few seconds.* Or words to that effect.

Lil sat on her hands and bit her lip in an effort to keep quiet. On the fifth try the engine spluttered into life and Abe wheel-spun away down the dirt track, snaking between the verges. They came to a stop at the gates in a screech of brakes and mud, waited for another car to pass by, and then Abe swung the wheel a sharp right and out onto the road to Peligan City.

Lil looked out through the side window at the city as they rattled towards it. She thought that the only time Peligan looked nice was at night, when the lights glittered in a latticework of orange, blue, pink and white – in other words, in the dark and from a distance.

'So, where are we headed?' she asked Abe. 'Are we going after Gallows?'

'Gallows is going after LeTeef,' Abe said grimly. 'If I knew where he was, I'd have gone after him myself. We'll never catch up with him now.'

Shivering from the rain and the adrenalin that was seeping away, they stared out of the windscreen. The wipers flapped wildly and the headlights caught the raindrops like stars plummeting past at light-speed.

'So are we just giving up?

'Have you got a better idea?'

A cold, creeping feeling slunk into the car and crawled over their skin, raising goose pimples and frosting their breath. With a sound like the last dregs of a milkshake being sucked up through a straw, Nedly appeared in the back seat.

'Gah!' Lil cried. Abe slammed on the brakes and they careened through a giant puddle and came to a stop.

'I take it he's back then,' Abe deduced.

Lil said nothing.

They sat there in silence but for the rain thumping on the metal roof and the tick-ticking of the engine until, unable to hold her tongue any longer, Lil blurted out angrily, 'Where have you been all this time? What were you doing that was so important that you abandoned us to get tied up, nearly burnt to a crisp and at the mercy of notorious murderer the Firebug ghost?'

Nedly tried to explain. 'I was finding out what Gallows' next move would be, so we could go after him when you escaped.'

'Assuming we escaped at all.'

'I sent Owl to rescue you.' Nedly winced sheepishly. 'I know that sounds risky, but it was a calculated risk. Leonard Owl isn't a cold-blooded killer. I mean, he did set those fires and kill those people, but only because Gallows made him do it.'

Lil arched an eyebrow at him in a *whatever*.

'So we swapped places, me and Owl. He went after you – to rescue you,' Nedly corrected himself. 'While I stuck to Gallows to find out what his next move was going to be. He can't tell one ghost from another so he assumed I was his henchman and let me in on the whole show. I thought you'd be pleased.'

'So . . . ?'

'So?' Nedly echoed her uncertainly.

'So, what is his next move?'

Abe cleared his throat noisily. 'Have you forgotten I'm here?'

'What's that?' said Lil; she *had* forgotten he was there. 'Sorry, no, of course not. Nedly was just saying that he knows what Gallows is planning.'

Abe huffed. 'He's going after LeTeef; he told us that much himself.'

'But you don't know where he's gone because *you* don't know who LeTeef is.' Nedly's eyes gleamed in the faraway light of the burning asylum. 'But I do.'

Lil reported back to Abe. 'Nedly says he knows where Ramon LeTeef is.'

'What!' Abe exclaimed. 'Where is he?'

Nedly looked Lil square in the face and said with authority. 'Not where. Who. He's the mayor, Tantalus Dean.'

'No!' Lil gasped. '*Really?*'

Abe tapped loudly on the dashboard to get Lil's attention. 'I didn't hear him. Where is he?'

Nedly nodded gravely. 'He's been hiding in plain sight all this time.'

Lil shook her head. 'I can't believe it.'

Abe tried to butt in again. 'What can't you believe?'

'Believe it,' Nedly told her. 'It makes perfect sense – that's why the Firebug was after him, *and* why he covered up the attack. He couldn't risk being identified with the Lucan Road Mob victims.'

'And the way he reacted to you in the corridor,' Lil chipped in, warming to the idea. 'He'd been haunted before, that's why he panicked. Remember? Mum said she had to save him by putting out a fire. When he felt your presence he must have thought you were the same ghost back again to finish him off – that's why he freaked out so much . . . It all fits.'

'Hey!' Abe yelled. 'I'm still in the dark here!'

'I keep forgetting he can't hear you,' Lil explained to Nedly.

'No, I can't hear him,' Abe fumed. 'So do you mind telling me what's going on?'

'I keep forgetting you can't hear him,' Lil explained to Abe.

'I realise that,' he said through gritted teeth. 'So?'

'So.' Lil shrugged. 'I'm sorry.'

'No!' Abe's face was puce. 'I mean: so, where – is – he?

Lil paused dramatically and then, noticing that Abe's eye had started to twitch dangerously and might actually pop out if she kept him in suspense much longer, she let the words just tumble out: 'The man you've been looking for all these years, it's the mayor – Tantalus Dean.'

Abe's jaw dropped an inch. For a moment he seemed lost for words, and then he found one. 'Impossible!'

'Not impossible.' Lil flicked his disbelief aside. 'Think about it, Abe. The two most distinctive characteristics about Ramon LeTeef are his white hair and his yellow pointed teeth, right? And even though the mayor is in his forties, his hair doesn't have any grey in it, not a speck. So maybe he dyes it! And if you think about it, his teeth do kind of stick out. So, maybe they are false teeth! And why would someone dye their hair and wear false teeth? Well, maybe it's because they are trying to disguise the two things that would make them conspicuous!'

Lil gave Abe a moment to let the revelation soak in. She watched him chew it over, clenching and unclenching his jaw, while breathing heavily through his nose.

'Don't sweat it, Abe,' she said helpfully. 'I didn't notice either. I suppose it's like one of those optical illusions; you either see it or you don't. Of course, once you do, it is *so* obvious.'

Abe let his forehead drop onto the steering wheel. 'I've been searching for LeTeef for years and he was right there, under my nose, all along. I don't deserve to be called a detective.'

'Come off it!' cried Lil. 'No one knew! Well, I'll bet Weasel did – that's probably why he came after you at the Mingo. When he saw you in the lobby of City Hall that time he must have thought you were on to them. No wonder this city is going down the toilet; the mayor is a dangerous crook – and a dead one if we don't hurry up. Let's go!'

Abe crunched the car into gear and they pulled away at speed.

'So where does the mayor live?' asked Lil.

'Beats me,' said Abe.

Lil looked askance at Nedly but he just shrugged back.

'OK,' said Lil. 'Pull up over there.' She pointed towards an isolated phone box further up the road.

She jumped out and into a puddle, barely pausing to angrily kick some of the water off the surface. Her fingers were wet and slippery as she flicked through the fat telephone directory looking for Dean, T.

Lil found it tucked away amongst the thin grey pages, in micro-typeface, but there for all to see. She bolted back to the car and stretched her seat belt across her lap. 'It's 211, Yang Guang Heights.'

'Of course it is,' growled Abe.

He did an eight-point turn on the narrow country lane and then they sped off as Lil pulled a Peligan City A–Z out of the glove compartment and started shouting directions over the roar of the engine.

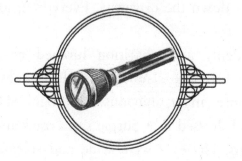

Chapter 25

Chez Dean

Yang Guang Heights was Peligan's playground for the rich and infamous, a luxury estate in the Garden District on the north side of town. The mansion houses were designed to resemble the imperial palaces of ancient China, with green and sweeping gabled roofs and winged balconies that encircled each floor.

Number 211 stood back from the road amidst sloping lawns and glassy rectangular ponds. The electric gates were already open. Abe switched the lights to low and rolled the car slowly down the driveway. Everything looked quiet. Too quiet.

Suddenly an apparition lurched past the headlights. Abe slammed on the brakes, but the figure ran on, oblivious. Lil recognised Craig Weasel dressed in a purple satin tracksuit and sandals. His eyes were wide and staring, his mouth was agape and his hair streamed behind him like ginger string.

Abe and Lil exchanged glances.

'It looks like the party has already started,' Abe noted grimly, and then he moved the car forward again. They pulled up outside the front door and he killed the lights. The house was in darkness.

Lil looked nervously at the mansion, and then back down the drive where Craig Weasel had fled. 'Maybe the storm caused a power cut?'

'Maybe,' said Abe. He rubbed at the stubble on his chin. 'You wait out here for me. I'm going in alone.'

Nedly gave Lil a worried look. 'The other

ghost, Mr Grip, is probably inside. I'll be able to see him, but you won't. Neither will Abe. He'll be a sitting duck.'

'We'll stick together,' Lil informed Abe. 'Either we all go in, or no one does.'

'I don't suppose I could stop you anyway,' he grumbled. 'All right, but don't take any chances. Ramon LeTeef is a dangerous man, and so is Gallows. What we potentially have here is a situation involving two dangerous criminals in a dark and unfamiliar house, and if what Gallows said was true, another ghost that we can neither see nor hear but who may attack us at any time.'

Abe switched his driving attachment for his multi-purpose pincers, slipped a monkey wrench into the pocket of his mac and strung a pair of binoculars round his neck. Lil zipped up her mac and stuffed a notebook and pencil into her pocket.

'You've got your tools of the trade; I've got mine,' she said, scooping up the torch from the foot well.

They got out of the car and quietly closed the doors. Abe held out his hand.

'Give me the torch.'

'It's OK, I've got it.'

'It's my torch.'

Lil puffed out her cheeks. 'What does it matter who carries it? Fine, you take it if it means that much to you.' She pushed it at him.

'Thanks.' Abe gripped it firmly. 'It does.'

He moved the beam of light across the front of the house, dipping it into the empty rooms. It didn't look like anyone was home. Lil nudged Abe and pointed towards the back of the house where a cloud of smoke was rising into the night air.

'Over there,' she said.

They hurried towards it. The smoke was coming from a log-cabin-style outbuilding. As they drew nearer they realised it wasn't smoke, but steam that was billowing out through the open door of the mayor's private sauna. Lil peeked inside; there was no sign of the mayor.

Abe pinned himself against the wall of the

house and gestured for Lil to wait there, then poked at the back door. It swung open with a creak onto a dark and empty utility room.

'All right,' said Abe. He paused on the threshold. 'Stay behind me.'

'I'll go first,' said Nedly, and slipped through the brickwork.

Inside, the air was colder than it was outside. Abe's torchlight quivered along the walls like a nervous search beam checking each room for adversaries, alive or dead. In the conservatory, draughts fluttered the leaves of waxy plants and rattled blinds. They went through to the kitchen, where a line of hanging cups swayed and knocked against each other and the taps groaned and trickled.

As they made their way along the hall – *bang!* – a door slammed shut somewhere. Abe spun his torch round to face the direction of the sound and the bulb flickered and grew dim.

The detective gulped audibly.

Lil's breath billowed out in front of her like a cloud of fog. 'Why do you think Gallows called the other ghost Mr Grip?' she asked shakily.

Abe's fingers instinctively reached for his throat. 'I don't think I want to know.'

'Because that's how he kills people,' Nedly answered in a voice so quiet that it was less than a whisper. 'He strangles them. Owl told me.'

'I don't think I wanted to know that either,' muttered Lil. She reached out a hand and took hold of Abe's sleeve.

'Something's coming,' he growled.

They looked up as the sound of scampering footsteps danced overhead and then faded into another part of the house. The door at the end of the hall was shut but they could hear a scraping sound and then a thud coming from beyond it.

'Stay close,' whispered Abe, as they shuffled reluctantly onwards. 'I think he's in there.' He turned the handle and the door itself swung open with a reedy screech revealing a darkened room that smelt of cigar smoke.

Cold sweat beaded Lil's forehead as she cautiously followed Abe inside and beckoned Nedly to come too.

He peered over her shoulder. 'I think I can see someone standing there in the darkness.'

Now that her eyes had adjusted Lil could just make out the ghostly form too. She tugged at Abe's sleeve and tried to say something but only a high-pitched squeak came out.

Abe swung the torchlight up and they both gasped, staggering back. Abe tripped over a coffee table and dropped the torch. The light went out.

While he tried to scramble to his feet Lil groped around until she found the torch and then, with hands shaking, fumbled the switch until the light came on. She pointed it like a weapon at the figure.

It was a statue of Mayor Dean, an alabaster figure with a much-exaggerated physique and an election-winning smile. Lil breathed out in relief and dropped the beam but caught something else. Something that shrank back from the light like a spider.

They could hear the gibbering, whispering sound the thing was making as it crouched in the corner. Lil caught it in the torch beam again. Mayor Dean, aka Ramon LeTeef, was huddled behind the statue, his scrawny arms and legs cradling his pot belly. He was wearing nothing but skimpy blue swimming trunks and a pair of brown-glass tanning goggles strung round his neck. His eyes wheeled round, blinking in the strong light. His false teeth were gone and his mouth was full of pointed and glistening yellow teeth. His bloodshot eyes quivered, and beneath his fake tan Lil could see that his face was grey and clammy.

'Help me,' he whispered, and then he fainted.

Abe caught his body as it collapsed forward. He shook LeTeef hard and then gave him a sharp slap to the chops. The mayor came around with a woozy expression.

'Ramon LeTeef,' Abe said, strong-arming the mostly naked man to his feet. 'At last, we meet again.'

He was about to embark on what Lil imagined was a well-rehearsed speech when LeTeef suddenly cocked his head to one side, as though he had heard something in the air. Then, without warning, he wriggled free and, shrieking blue murder, ran from the room with his bare feet slip-slapping on the tiled floor.

'What the . . . ?' Abe cursed and turned to follow but the door LeTeef had just exited through slammed shut in his face.

The torchlight was snuffed out like a candle flame. Lil started shaking; her heart was hammering in her chest. From somewhere far away they heard the distant sound of bells tinkling. Abe rummaged in his pockets for a matchbook and after a couple of strikes a yellow flame sprang to life at the end of a shaking pincer.

His face was marble-white and sweat trickled down from his hat. 'I don't like this,' he said. The match went out.

They heard a sound from the hallway, a lurching creak, a heavy weight shifting on a floorboard.

Abe lit another match; he looked over at Lil. Lil was watching Nedly.

'He's coming,' Nedly whispered. 'Mr Grip.'

'We have to get out of here,' Abe barked, but when he saw the look on Lil's face he froze. 'What? What is it?'

Creeeak. This time it sounded nearer. *Creeeak*. The footsteps paused. They all stared at the door as very slowly the knob began to turn.

Lil just had time to murmur, 'Do you see that?' when the second match went out as an icy draught filled the room.

Creeeak. Abe lit his third and final match. As it flared, they watched in horror as the door swung open. No one was there. Lil and Abe exchanged uncertain glances but Nedly staggered backwards, his wide-eyed gaze tilted upwards at something no one else could see. The fine crystal teardrops on the chandelier tinkled softly.

'Is it him?' Lil couldn't stop her voice from trembling.

Silently Nedly nodded his head.

The matchlight danced in Abe's shaking hand. Shadows jumped on the walls.

'What's he doing?'

Nedly's eyes didn't move from the point he was fixed on. His voice was barely a whisper. 'He's just standing there, staring.'

Lil waited a beat. 'Is he still standing there?'

'No.'

'Where is he now?'

Nedly turned his head slowly to face her. Lil could see the answer from the look in his eyes. There was a heavy *creeeak!* from nearby and then the third match went out.

'Lil?' Abe hissed at her from across the room.

Lil stood motionless in the abysmal dark, her heart beating like a boxer on a speed bag. In the blackness pixelated, vague shapes coalesced into thicker shadows, amassing in the centre of the room, moving towards her and becoming a thing she could not see but somehow sense, as empty and as terrible as a black hole.

Time seemed to stand still. Lil's breath abandoned her as a faint wisp that curled away and then was suddenly blown to pieces as the lit-up and shimmering form of Nedly burst from the shadows and skidded to a halt in front of her. His thin frame seemed to block the terrible darkness ahead. Lil stumbled backwards and watched, horror-struck, as Nedly launched himself at the invisible bulk of Mr Grip and gave him a massive shove.

Books flew off shelves, glass smashed against walls, and the mirror exploded. The radiogram sprang to life in a display of lights and sound, making them all jump. At ear-splitting volume a chirpy song rang out: *Don't sit under the apple tree with anyone else but me, anyone else but me, anyone else but me. No, no, no.* And then the speakers blew but the music continued, only now the song was playing backwards.

Crouching on the floor, Lil could just see Nedly, his pale skin still glowing white, leaning with all his might and somehow holding the colossal ghost at bay. No, not just holding him at bay – from the angle of his body Lil realised he was actually forcing him backwards. Nedly was winning.

The walls groaned, the ceiling cracked and with a metallic snap the large chandelier broke free from its chains, plummeted straight through Nedly and hit the ground with a crash, sending up a spray of crystal, which pelted Lil like hail.

'Lil!' she heard Abe shout, adding to the din as he hurtled his way towards her through the chaos, tripping over rugs and footstools, wading through scatter cushions, never slowing until, finally, he struck out and found her, crawled over to where she was huddled and formed a shield against the flying debris. He took a battering through his worn old mac, which tented out like a cloak around them, with one arm crooked overhead to try to fend off an enemy he couldn't see.

From under the mac Lil could see Nedly standing his ground, like a twig resisting a gale-force wind, but it seemed to her that he was growing dull and flickering – and had his feet shifted position slightly to a more defensive stance? *He's getting tired*, she thought and realised with horror that he was starting to lose. She wanted to yell at him to give up and get out of there, but he was their only hope of getting away. Wishing that there was something, anything, she could do to help him fight, Lil put all her frustration into the only weapon she had left and above the chaos and the noise she shouted, 'COME ON, NEDLY! COME ON!'

Nedly burnt brighter. The three-piece suite exploded, cushions ripping, sending a fountain of feathers into the air. Through the dust and stuffing Lil could see his skinny form arched over, like he was forcing a lid shut on an impossibly full suitcase. His arms were trembling with the effort. His eyes were glaring white.

'COME ON, NEDLY!' Abe bellowed suddenly into the wilderness. 'YOU CAN DO IT!'

The lanky ghost of Ned Stubbs, lit up like a flare, shoved back against the floor with his legs and then tumbled forward, as though a door he had been pushing against had finally swung open. The radiogram cut out. The other ghost had gone.

It was over – just like that.

Nedly clambered to his feet, and stood bent over, his hands resting on his knees. He looked drained and so thin he was almost concave. He looked up at Lil with a mystified almost-smile on his lips. 'You OK?'

Lil snorted. 'I'm OK. Are *you* OK?'

'I'm OK,' answered Abe shakily.

Nedly nodded slowly. 'I think so. I can't believe . . .' The words were snatched away as he was suddenly yanked backwards as if someone had taken hold of a fistful of sweatshirt and jerked him off his feet. One minute he was falling and then there was a sucking sound like a plunger on a drain and the ghost of Ned Stubbs disappeared.

Hearing Lil scream, Abe screamed too. Then they both stood in darkness and silence.

'What just happened?' Abe croaked.

'He's vanished! Nedly! Gone!' The words spilled out as panic whirred in Lil's belly. She struggled to piece together what she had just witnessed. 'I think he's taken him.'

'Who's taken who?'

'Mr Grip has taken Nedly.' She couldn't believe it.

They were dazzled as the house lights suddenly blinked on, followed by the garden lanterns and then security floodlights that illuminated the driveway. Lil felt the temperature in the room start to rise and the creepy feeling that had shot through the house began to dissipate. She had never been so sorry to feel normal.

The old detective clambered to his feet and shook the splinters of glass and crockery from his mac. He held out a hand and pulled Lil back onto her feet. 'Come on, kid. We've got work to do. If Nedly has taken out this other ghoul, then he's bought us a window of opportunity to apprehend LeTeef.'

Lil stared up at him miserably.

Abe didn't meet her eye. 'I'm sure he'll be back,' he said, roughing up a patch of paisley-patterned rug underfoot.

'You better be right,' Lil muttered gloomily.

They found LeTeef in an upstairs bathroom,

hiding in the tub. He had pulled the shower curtain down and it hung over him like a ghostly sheet, but without any eyeholes. Lil could hear him whimpering to himself.

'I never meant to betray you, Cornelius; I was always going to come back . . .' His voice had a strangled tone. 'But then there was the fire, and I thought, I thought . . . But you can still have your slice; you can have the whole pie, if you want it! Although it's tied up in investments at the moment. I could give you a deposit . . . ? You could have my car . . . my . . . my . . . Hello?' he whispered, suddenly aware of their presence. 'Is . . . anybody there?'

Abe snatched the curtain away and towered over his prey, his jaw set, his eyes steely grey with a hint of triumph.

LeTeef shrieked and threw a sponge at Abe. He had put his tanning goggles on and Lil could see his eyes bulging behind them, transfixed with terror as he watched Abe pull a thick white towelling robe off the back of the door and throw it at him.

'Put this on, I'm taking you in.'

LeTeef obeyed. He was still shivering even with the robe. He clambered out of the bath tub and staggered away from the detective as if some instinct was still telling him to run but when he reached the door he recoiled from it. He looked bewildered, as though he couldn't work out where the greater danger lay. In the end his fear of the supernatural overpowered his fear of the law. He turned on the spot, and ran back towards Abe, slipping over on the lino with a painful slap. He climbed up onto his knees, cringing.

'Don't leave me here,' pleaded LeTeef, his hands held out for handcuffs that Abe no longer possessed. Instead Abe reached out with his good hand and pulled the ex-mayor to his feet.

'What's the matter with him?' said Lil, as LeTeef clung to Abe's mac, huddling against the detective's bulk as a child would its mother.

'He's been scared out of his wits,' said Abe. 'Whatever he faced here, he thinks he'll be safer in jail.'

'He won't be, though, will he?' whispered Lil as Abe led LeTeef down the stairs and out of the house towards the Zodiac.

'No, but if that's what he wants . . . I'm happy to oblige.'

Chapter 26

Is This Justice?

A day later the *Klaxon* ran the exposé; it was a special edition written in memory of A. J. McNair.

Years of Mob Rule at City Hall Finally at an End!

Mayor Dean has been relieved of office and arrested pending charges after being exposed as former mobster Ramon LeTeef, the notorious criminal who disappeared

into the Witness Protection Programme over a decade ago, following the botched trial of the Lucan Road Mob.

A mountain of hard evidence, collected as part of a long undercover operation by the Klaxon's own investigative team, was presented to the Prosecutor's Office early this morning. In response, Peligan City law-enforcement officials have had no choice but to apprehend the former mayor and seize all his official and personal financial records from City Hall. This included documents relating to money-laundering scams, incidences of corporate fraud, insider dealings and election rigging. It is hoped that these documents will be used to make the case against LeTeef and identify some of his associates, former gangsters turned local business tycoons and politicians. As a result several top officials are in line to lose their jobs and contracts. The incriminating paperwork substantiates the allegations that our own

reporter Randall Collar has made previously in his column, the Rotten Barrel.

Additional material has also been recovered overnight from the former mayor's residence at Yang Guang Heights. This includes a ledger that records criminal interactions with City Hall from back during Al Davious's term. The retired ex-mayor Davious is now being sought for questioning.

Police commissioner Gordian has been brought in to investigate the extent of the corruption at the heart of Peligan's political system and the city's assets have been frozen while this goes on.

Thanks to some crusading work carried out by the team at Mandrel Investigations and the endeavours of our own undercover reporters the mob rule at City Hall has finally come to an end.

After they had finished at the police station, Abe walked Lil back to the corner of Angel

Lane. His car had been re-impounded when he had delivered LeTeef up to the duty sergeant.

'Some thanks that is,' Abe had complained, handing over the keys.

'You're lucky we're not bringing charges against you for stealing it, Mandrel,' the sergeant had replied, but he winked at the same time.

'Looks like I took the rap for you there, kid,' said Abe when they got clear of the station. 'Officially, if anyone stole my car it was you.'

'I only liberated it,' said Lil with a half-hearted attempt at a grin.

Abe slanted a look at her. 'Chin up, kid. I know you miss him.'

Lil shrugged. She'd had a bit of grit in her eye all day.

'Collar beat me to the exposé,' she said ruefully. 'At least we got a mention, though.' She folded her copy of the *Klaxon* carefully and stowed it in her rucksack. 'This story is going to blow City Hall wide open. Apparently they're already calling for a new election.

'So, what will happen to LeTeef now?'

'He is being transferred to the Secure Wing for the Criminally Insane at the Needle. The new consultant there, Dr Lankin, has agreed to admit LeTeef while he's awaiting trial. Interestingly enough, Lankin used to work with Carvel at Rorschach too so he was probably on Gallows' hit list as well.'

'Maybe he still is. You should warn him.'

'Maybe so,' conceded Abe. 'But I'm not sure he'd believe me.'

'How about Weasel? Can they get him for aiding and abetting or whatever?'

'A patrol car picked him up on the highway not far from Yang Guang. He was gibbering. No doubt he'll have plenty to say once the creeps wear off, but my guess is he'll try for a plea bargain. The cops are going to be under pressure to put LeTeef away for good this time, and if justice is served Weasel will go right down with him.'

Lil bit her lip. 'Did you take care of that other thing?'

Abe nodded gravely. 'An anonymous tip-off. The scene-of-crime fellas will do a thorough search of the grounds at Rorschach. They'll find him.'

'Good.' Lil stared down at her shoes. 'One day I'd like to tell the whole story: what happened to Nedly before he died and afterwards. I suppose it would be kind of hard to substantiate it, the stuff with Gallows and Owl, and Mr Grip and all that.' She sniffed. 'And maybe it would be hard to believe it too, but I owe it to Nedly to try. He was pretty brave, you know?'

'He was a real hero.'

'He was. I'm glad I got to know him, just a little bit.' Lil swallowed back the lump in her throat, and after a moment changed the subject. 'So what will you do now that LeTeef has been found? Have you got any other cases to work on?'

'I suppose I'll have to track down Gallows at some point,' said Abe grimly. 'I get the feeling he isn't done with Peligan City yet.'

'You'll get him.'

'You bet I'll give it a shot.'

Lil looked at Abe with a critical eye. His mac was drenched and black with soot, his tie was loose and his shirt had seen better days. 'Well, if you need any help . . .'

'I'll know where to come.' He cranked out a rusty smile and nodded towards the window of number ten. 'Looks like your tea's almost ready.'

Lil had half expected the house to be empty as usual but as she peered through the window past the door of the dark sitting room and into the glow of the kitchen she could see her mum frantically trying to cook dinner, which, she predicted, would be spaghetti bolognese with garlic bread. 'It's her "speciality",' she told Abe.

'I remember.' He looked wistful.

The sound of an approaching train filled the night air, rattling past in a thunder of noise. A hot wind gusted behind it, whipping strands of hair across Lil's face. After the sound had faded away and the few skittering leaves that had been pulled in its wake finally came to rest, all that was left was the faint lull of a lady singing the blues percolating out into the street from the old record player on the sideboard.

Lil could smell the sweet tomato sauce on the evening air and thought, for the first time in a long while, that it was good to be home. 'Hey, do you want to come in for a bite?'

There was no reply. The old detective was already halfway down the road and out of earshot. As he passed beyond the street lamp he raised a hand in a wave until he became no more than a shadow in a hat and mackintosh.

Naomi Potkin's eyes were sparkling happily. She reached out a hand to ruffle Lil's hair and then pulled her in for a bear hug. 'I'm sorry I haven't been around much lately, but that big project I was working on – it's finished, so maybe we can spend a bit more time together. If you want?'

Lil shrugged like it didn't matter but said, 'OK.'

Her mother nodded at the kitchen table. 'This arrived for you.'

She stepped aside to reveal a box-shaped parcel wrapped in dirty newspaper and string. Lil pulled on the bow and grinned widely. The paper opened to reveal an old but unused Olympia SM-3 typewriter. A couple of keys were half melted, it needed a new ribbon and the platen was still a bit sooty around the edges, although someone had hurriedly given it a once-over with a damp cloth. There was a card stuck between the rows of letters. It read: 'You might as well have this. Abe'.

The food was good and Lil ate as much as she could fit in her belly, but she couldn't shake off the dark cloud that hung over her that night.

Alone in her room she stared grimly at the silhouette portrait of A. J. McNair. She pinned back the foxed corner and smoothed it down, pressing against the sticky tack that held it in place.

'Hi,' she said awkwardly. 'It's me again. Feels like long time no see.' The profile stared blankly ahead. Lil tried again. 'You'll never guess what happened.' It wasn't the same; the picture just seemed like a picture: two-dimensional and disinterested.

She carefully cut out the front-page news article from the special-edition *Klaxon* and pinned that up there too and then she switched off the light and listened in the darkness. Behind the soft swell of the blues, which was still drifting up from two floors below, the night seemed eerily still and there was a definite chill in the air.

'Nedly?' she whispered hopefully.

No answer.

Lil crept over to the window. It was slightly open. She heard the hum of a train in the distance; the noise vibrated against the latch as she pulled it shut. The train tore past, into the night, with a shunting heartbeat and lonely-sounding honk, while Lil stared out into the street, through the rain, past the street lamps and the houses. She leant closer to the glass, peering out over the city, past the lights of the tramlines, past the prison, to the black of the night sky. Then, taking a deep breath, she let it out in a sigh.

The window misted up before her.

'Nedly?' she said again, closing her eyes and screwing them shut.

Slowly she prised her lids open. She was still alone.

'Nedly, if you can hear me, come back.'

She stood there holding the cord that lowered the blind, ready to pull it down, but hesitating. *Come back*, she thought, *even if it's just to say goodbye*.

A sound rippled through the night, like a fat drop of water hitting a full bath tub. Lil strained her eyes against the fuzzy darkness. Far down the road a speck emerged from round the sweep of the corner. The speck became a small figure, and then the figure became a boy. He was racing determinedly through the slanting rain without disturbing the puddles, and passing under street lamps without casting a shadow. When he reached number ten Angel Lane he came to a stop, and waited patiently in the rain for someone to open the door and let him in.

By the time she had put on her dressing gown and slippers and crept down the two flights of stairs as quickly and quietly as her feet would carry her, some of Lil's tearful excitement had worn off, so that by the time she reached the front door the first thing she thought to say was: 'Why didn't you just come in?'

'You know why.' Nedly rolled his eyes, puffed out his cheeks and then deflated them with a powerful sigh. 'I told you: it's not a good feeling moving through solid objects.'

'But if I hadn't been looking out of the window at that moment, I wouldn't even have known you were there and then you would have been waiting all night.'

'But I saw you standing at the window so I knew you had seen me.'

Lil opened her mouth to argue back and then

370

shut it with a lopsided smile. 'Whatever. It's very good to see you, Nedly.'

He returned the grin. 'It's good to see you too.'

'You made it back. I knew you would. I knew Grip was no match for you.'

Nedly's smile flickered and went out with a gulp. He twitched a quick glance over his shoulder and Lil noticed his eyes had a round and stretched look to them.

'Anyway,' she said, stepping aside, 'come in. Welcome home!'

'Thanks.' Nedly gave her a bashful shrug as he passed. 'It's good to be back.'

Lil paused in the doorway for a moment, wrapping her dressing gown tight. The night had an icy edge to it. The nearest street lamp buzzed and grew dim, making the shadows in the alley opposite thicken into something darker than black.

Listening to her own heartbeat pulsing in her ears, Lil wondered if maybe she had just forgotten what the creeps felt like. *Well*, she thought brightly, *I better get used to them again,* and, shaking them off with a sudden shudder, she gave the empty street a good dose of the Penetrating Squint for luck and then turned inside and closed the door.

Acknowledgements

Emma Matthewson, Jenny Jacoby and all the good people at Piccadilly Press; agent extraordinaire, Hilary Delamere; Fay Davies; Holly Tonks; Jessica Hare; Caroline Ambrose, the junior judges, and the readers at the Bath Novel Award; Ann Halliday for the shake up; Faye Sheldrake for never giving up; fellow writers Francesca Armour-Chelu, Liz Ferretti, Ruth Dugdall, Morag Liffen and Jane Bailey for the advice and support. Early readers Julia

Billington and Jane Baker; Nick Smith for the website; Graham Felce and Kellie Dimmock for the photographs; MJ Mahoney for the book recommendations, Richard Baker for the music and Dorothy B Hughes for the inspiration.

This has been a long road and plenty of people have helped me along it: Nicki, Margaret, Betty, Dave, Yves, Tom, Lizzy, Gene and Cara – thanks a million.

Sophie Green

Sophie Green writes children's fiction, short stories and scripts. She has a degree in zoology and an interest in folklore. She was born and still lives in Suffolk and works in a public library.

Her first novel, *The Last Giant*, was shortlisted for the *Times*/Chicken House Children's Fiction Competition in 2011. Her short stories have been highly commended for the Bridport Prize 2012, longlisted for BBC Opening Lines in 2013 and 2015 and won second prize in Words with Jam in 2014. Her story *Potkin and Stubbs* was recently shortlisted for the Bath Children's Novel Award.

Karl James Mountford

Karl James Mountford was born in Germany and is now a full-time illustrator based in Wales.

He studied illustration at Swansea College of Art and was also the artist in residence there while studying for his M.A. in Visual Communication.

He now spends most of his day illustrating all types of awesome stories and genres.

Piccadilly
P R E S S

Thank you for choosing a Piccadilly Press book.

If you would like to know more about our authors, our books or if you'd just like to know what we're up to, you can find us online.

www.piccadillypress.co.uk

You can also find us on:

We hope to see you soon!